Easy As Pie, Until Someone Dies

Janet McNulty

Easy As Pie, Until Someone Dies

Copyright © 2020 Janet McNulty
Cover Illustration by Robert Henry
Interior Text Design by Janet McNulty

ISBN-13: 978-1-941488-88-1
ISBN-10: 1-941488-88-9

Printed in the United States of America

*For all those who ever had a cute and
cuddly boss known as a cat.*

Easy As Pie,
Until Someone Dies

Chapter 1

A strange noise woke me up. Well, it sort of woke me up as sleep still held onto me, encouraging me to close my eyes again, something that I wanted to do. I turned over, clenching the covers even tighter and drifted back to sleep. The same noise disturbed my peace again. Frustrated and annoyed, I rolled over again, doing my best to ignore the noisy neighbor in the hallway.

Meow!

I bolted upright, wide awake, knowing that there was no way I could go back to sleep now. Was that a cat I heard? There were no cats around here. I don't remember there being any cats, unless I ended up with a new neighbor who had one and it snuck out, mistaking my door for his.

Meow! Meow! Meow!

Okay. I couldn't just lay there in bed, ignoring a poor defenseless animal that had gotten lost. I threw the covers off. Yawning, I sat up, glancing at the clock. Four in the morning. It's too early to have to get up. I still had three more hours of sleep I could have gotten before having to start my Monday, get up and get to work. I stood up, still groggy and half-asleep, and shuffled out or my room, down the hallway, and to the door where the meowing came from.

Meow!

As the scratching and meowing at the door persisted, I yawned some more, still not fully awake and wishing I was in bed, under my warm covers. The wind howled outside. Looks like winter will be here early. I'm not ready for it. My feet scooted across the carpet, not wanting to open the door, but I couldn't ignore a lost cat. Its owner must be worried sick about it missing. I opened the door and a cat with blue eyes looked up at me, giving me an innocent look, while purring so loud, I swore that it would wake everyone else up.

"Mew," it said in a soft voice, so soft that I had trouble believing that it came from such a big cat. It has to be at least 15 pounds. Though most of that could be fur, and blueish-gray fur at that, which was so long that I imagined the hours it would take to brush it so that it didn't get all tangled and knotted.

The cat scurried past me and ran into the apartment, disappearing into the shadows. I shut the door and hurried after it. Where was it going? As though it knew where it was, it ran down the hallway and straight into my bedroom. Really? My bedroom? Geez, you'd think the thing lived here with the way it knew where to go. I hurried after it.

"Hey," I hissed at it, not wanting to wake Jackie and surprised that she was still sleeping, even though I was making enough noise to wake the dead.

I rushed into my room and stopped in the doorway. The cat laid on my bed,—in the middle of the bed as though it owned it—licking its butt. Its leg was stretched up in the air and the sounds of its tongue straightening its fur filled my once peaceful room. I didn't even know this cat, and it didn't know me, but here it was, making itself at home on my bed.

"Where am I supposed to sleep?" I asked.

The cat looked at me and curled up on the bed, putting its head on its front paw and closed its eyes. I walked over to my bed and picked the cat up, placing it on the floor and getting an angry meow in the process.

"This is my bed," I said to it.

It just glared at me as though it knew something I didn't.

I got into bed and pulled the covers up, hoping that I could get back to sleep and salvage what was left of my sleeping time. Before I could even finish getting comfortable, the cat jumped on the bed and curled up on the edge of my pillow, purring so loud that my eardrums vibrated. I've never had a cat before. Truth is, I've never had a pet before. My parents were against having pets, believing that they were messy and ruin furniture, so I had no idea what I was supposed to do with a cat that seemed to think that my bed was his. Not satisfied with being on my pillow, the cat walked over me, purring the entire time, and butted its head against my hand, nestling into to me. Not knowing what else to do, I rubbed its ears. It purred louder. The more the cat purred, the more I petted it, warming up to its presence. My hand brushed something around its neck. A collar. It felt strange. Even in the dark, I noticed something weird about the collar, but my eyes grew heavy and I couldn't keep them open. I'll worry about it in the morning.

I had just fallen asleep, with the cat snuggled next to me, when…

"Hey!"

I jumped, causing the cat to scream and run off.

Rachel sat by the side of my bed with a huge smile on her face and I groaned. Sleep. I just wanted some sleep. Was that too much to ask?

"So, after the zombie thing," Rachel said, unconcerned about the early morning hour, "the afterlife seems a little boring, so I thought I would stop by here. We can hang out! It's going to be fun!"

I buried my face into my pillow. Yep, it's Monday all right.

Chapter 2

Snores escaped my partially open mouth as spittle drooled from it, while my face remained buried in the pillow, despite the bit of sunshine that crept into the room. Something blared in my room, an annoying, incessant noise that attacked my eardrums, making me wish that it would shut up! Frustrated, I swung my arm and knocked the noise maker to the floor, which happened to be my alarm clock. Groaning, I lifted my head up as a line of spittle dangled from my mouth to my spit-soaked pillow.

"A little violent this morning, aren't you?" said a voice.

I turned my head. Rachel sat on my dresser staring at me with her arms folded. She loved to come and go from my life. Mostly she came into my life and hung around a bit, seeing just how much trouble she could get me into, not that I ever put up that much of a fight. My curiosity got me into a lot of trouble.

"Wow," Rachel continued, "you are not a morning person."

"What was your first clue?" I asked.

"You don't have to be nasty about it." Rachel jumped off the dresser, jostling it a bit for fun, and walked through the door. Did I mention that she was a ghost?

I stood up and stretched my back, trying to get the last remnants of sleep to disappear. Man, I'm exhausted. Getting woken up in the middle of the night for a… The cat! I had completely forgotten about the cat. Where was the cat? I looked around, but could find no sign of him. A part of me wondered if I had dreamed the whole thing or worse: started sleepwalking after having developed strange sleeping habits due to my tendency to get involved in unsolved murder cases.

I couldn't find the cat. It must have been a dream, but it felt so real. Knowing that I needed to get on with my day, I grabbed a clean shirt and jeans from my dresser and put them on after running a brush through my tangled hair. While still throwing my hair into a pony tail, I rushed out to the kitchen for some freshly brewed coffee that Jackie had just made. She poured herself a cup—I'm assuming it is her second for the morning—as I waked in.

"I was beginning to wonder if you were going to get up," she said, while I grabbed the pot of coffee and fixed myself a cup.

"Sorry," I said. "Some neighbor's cat woke me up last night, and I wasn't able to get back to sleep."

"Cat?" asked Jackie.

"Yeah. Didn't you hear it?"

"Nope." She took a sip of her coffee. "I didn't hear a thing."

"Seriously? It was meowing like crazy and loud enough to wake the dead."

"I don't know about that," Rachel said to me as Jackie shook her head in response to my question, "because I had no trouble sleeping."

"You don't need to sleep," I quipped at her.

Jackie raised an eyebrow as she stared at me over the top of her cup.

I sipped my coffee not wanting to talk to her, or answer her unspoken question: that we weren't alone, though she was kind of used to that by now, but whenever a ghost showed up, trouble wasn't too far behind.

I went to the fridge and pulled out a loaf of bread and some butter, preparing to make toast. Jackie continued to stare at me as I made some toast for a quick breakfast. I felt her eyes on me as a I buttered my toast and moved to the table with it and my coffee.

"Is there something you want to tell me?" she asked in a "I know something is going on" tone.

"Not really," I replied through a mouthful of buttery toast.

What could I tell her? That I thought I had heard a cat meowing last night, and it was so real that I actually saw the cat when I let it inside and it slept on my bed? Except, now the cat was missing, so it all must have been a dream. And, Rachel was here, again, because she liked dropping by for a visit.

"Mel?"

Jackie wasn't about to let it go. Not that I blame her.

"I told you," I said in an exasperated tone—I'm so exhausted—as I tried to remember what had happened last night, "I thought I heard a meowing at the door. I got up, opened the door, and in walked a cat. At least, I thought I saw a cat. So, I let it stay, thinking I would look for its owner when I got up this morning, but the cat is gone, you didn't hear anything, and… you haven't seen a cat, have you?"

"No," Jackie replied.

The microwave slowly opened behind Jackie, and I knew Rachel was behind it, trying to play a prank on her. Somehow, Jackie knew all about it, because she reached behind her and slammed it closed, causing Rachel to jump with a start.

"Hey!" Rachel whined so we both could hear her.

"Morning, Rachel," said Jackie as she finished her coffee.

"How'd you…" Rachel began.

"Stuff always moves around when you're here," Jackie replied. After all this time, she's gotten used to Rachel's presence to the point where it doesn't bother her anymore. "You need to find another way to get us."

Rachel frowned and stalked away with her arms crossed.

I finished my last bite of toast and chased it down with coffee. "Any plans after work today?" I asked.

"Not really. You?"

"Homework," I said.

I was still stuck with my dumb computer class, since the semester wasn't over yet. And my others were no better. With Thanksgiving coming up—it's only a few days away—finals weren't too far behind, and the professors had been piling on the homework. That, and Mr. Stilton had me working a few extra hours because of the impending holiday season. This is when we sell most of our candles and accessories. No wonder I'm exhausted.

The container of cream that had been left on the counter fell over, and the lid popped off, spilling cream all over the place.

Jackie jumped into action, grabbing some paper towels and wiping it up, though I think she smeared it more than cleaned it up. A towel hung in the air next to me. I took it, thanking Rachel, and hurried to the mess, wiping it up as best I could. Jackie and I both stopped. A portion of the cream had impressions being made into it as though something was trying to drink it. We both stared at it as Rachel came up behind us.

"I don't think your dream was a dream," Rachel said to me.

Jackie turned her head toward me. "You were saying something about a cat showing up."

I pointed at the milk being drunk by some invisible force.

"Hey," Rachel said, snapping her fingers, "they can't see you!"

Within seconds a Russian Blue cat appeared on the counter top, drinking the cream.

"Can ghost cats drink cream?" asked Jackie.

"I don't know," I said. "But remember that Halloween party where Rachel…"

"Let's not bring that up," Rachel interrupted me.

The cat stopped drinking the cream, licked its lips, and looked at us, wondering what we were staring at.

"So," said Jackie, "the cat you saw…"

"…was a ghost," I finished for her.

Of course, it was a ghost. I've read stories on the internet about people claiming to have felt the presence of a long-lost pet, but I've never experienced such a thing and did not understand why this cat would come to me. I've never owned a pet and have never seen this cat before. Why would it come here?

"Wait a minute." Jackie ran to her phone and picked it up, scrolling through it before showing it to me.

"What is it?" I asked.

She handed me her phone, and I took it, my eyes widening when I saw a picture of an old woman dressed in a long-sleeved dress with a frilly collar, holding a cat, one that looked just like the ghostly one on my countertop.

"I don't understand," I said. "Why would it come here?"

"Hello," Rachel thumped me on the head, pointing at herself.

"You brought it here?" I asked her.

"No!" Rachel replied.

"Then…" I began.

"Cuz you're a ghost magnet," Rachel said.

I scanned the article Jackie had shown me.

Patricia Paresgue, wife of the late George Paresgue, died early this morning in a violent car crash. Her car was found on Old Morehouse Road. Investigators believe that the car slid on the ice and Mrs. Paresgue lost control of the vehicle, and it overturned. There were two victims in last night's accident. Mrs. Paresgue's cat, Bentley, was also in the car. Neither survived.

My heart sank reading that last bit. I may not be much of a cat person, but I never liked it when animals died tragically, and this accident could have been avoided. The weather turned cold a few days ago, and we've had nothing but freezing rain ever since, conditions that no one should be driving in, if they can avoid it.

Wait a minute. The cat—Bentley showed up at my door at around four in the morning. If he died in the car accident, then that means that Mrs. Paresgue was driving at around that time—awfully early for an old woman to be driving around and well before the sun comes up. Judging by the pearls around her neck, and the sapphire earrings she wore in the photo the local news decided to include in the article, I don't think she worked, so why was she out so early and in such bad weather.

"Uh oh," Jackie said, her eyes narrowing.

"What?" I asked.

"I know that look."

"What look?" I have a look?

"You don't think it was an accident," Jackie said in an accusatory tone.

"I didn't say anything," I protested.

"You don't have to," Jackie said. "You get the same look on your face every time you think that something isn't the way it seems."

"She's right," Rachel added.

"I don't…" I began. "Okay, think about it. The cat showed up at the door at around four in the morning. It died in the car accident. That means that this Mrs. Paresgue was driving in the freezing rain at around that time. Why would anyone be out that early and in such terrible weather? Look at the way she is dressed. Does this look like a woman going to work so early in the morning?"

Both Jackie and Rachel shook their heads, while Bentley stared at me with a look that said it was about time I realized the reason for him being here.

I glanced at the clock in the room. Was that the time? I'm ten minutes late for work!

"Oh my God we are so late!" I yelled, pointing at the clock. Jackie snatched her phone and ran to her bedroom to grab her purse, while I scooped up my keys and phone from the table near the door. Mr. Stilton is going to fire us for sure.

We both ran for the door and collided as we tried to get out at the same time, while Rachel laughed in the background. I stopped.

"What is so funny?" I asked.

"You guys," Rachel said through a burst of laughter.

I glared at her.

"I pushed all the clocks ahead by ten minutes. How's that for an early morning prank?"

Jackie's face turned red, and I didn't blame her. She started for Rachel, but I grabbed her arm and stopped her.

"Won't do much good," I said. "She's already dead."

"And loving it!" laughed Rachel.

"Keep an eye on Bentley," I told her as I pushed Jackie out the door and we hurried down the hall to the exit, trying not to be late for work.

Chapter 3

Jackie and I arrived at the Candle Shoppe just in time for the start of our shift, for which I was grateful. Changing the clocks like that. It wasn't even April Fool's yet. Oh dear! What will Rachel do for April Fool's? I dreaded the thought of the prank she had up her sleeve for that day, knowing that she would do something.

Jackie and I hurried to the door, knowing that there shouldn't be anyone in the store, since we weren't open yet. We stopped. Tammy was outside bending over a God-awful display of feathers, hay, painted eggs, and... a cat scratcher? What in the...

"Tammy!" Jackie blurted out, startling me from my internal dialogue about this display of hers. "What is all this?"

Tammy turned around, and it took every bit of

will-power I had to not laugh at her outfit. Her shirt jostled with every movement she made and looked like it was a bunch of leaves sewn on there,—I'm sure they were just something she had cut out and fashioned herself— and each little movement made them bounce around, which did not look good when they reached her bosom. Seriously, she looked like a chicken in that outfit. Her pants weren't so bad. They looked like some bellbottoms she got from a thrift store and had a yellow ribbon twisting up and down both legs, which looked tasteful compared to the travesty of her shirt.

Jackie started to laugh, but I put my hand over her mouth to get her to stop. She glared at me, and I glared back. Two of us can play that game.

"I thought I would help you with the display," Tammy said in an innocent tone.

"By taking it over?" asked Jackie.

Mr. Stilton had wanted a Thanksgiving display put up and had tasked Jackie with setting it up, but it seems that Tammy had decided to just do it herself. This isn't the first time her impulsiveness caused her to do such a thing. I still remembered that July Fourth display she had helped me with by using real fireworks. That was a disaster and she would have been fired if it wasn't for Rachel convincing Mr. Stilton to let her keep her job. She hadn't been so bad lately, at least, not after I had her organize the backroom, and she had shown considerable skill at doing such a thing, but sometimes her impulsiveness reared its ugly head. This was one of those times.

"Are you…" Jackie began, but I cut her off.

"She does appreciate your helpfulness," I said to Tammy, "but you should have asked her first, since this was her responsibility."

Tammy hung her head. She didn't seem too hurt, and I wasn't trying to hurt her feelings. She just needed to learn to ask before doing whatever entered her mind.

"Sorry," she whispered.

I looked at Jackie. She continued to scowl at Tammy, until I raised both my eyebrows as a way of telling her to say something nice.

"Apology accepted," said Jackie in a bored tone.

"One question: why is this outside?" I asked. Our displays are always inside so that way they don't get damaged from the weather.

"That's your only question?" Jackie said to me.

I waved her off.

"It's so nice out," said Tammy, "and this way, we can attract more customers."

I looked at the sky. It was nice and sunny now, but it had rained earlier and there were clouds in the distance. At this time of year, the weather could change quickly and often. "You might want to pack this up and bring it inside," I told her as I headed for the door and let myself in, with Jackie right behind me.

"I cannot believe her!" Jackie fumed.

I tried to quiet her. "Mr. Stilton might be in his office," I reminded her.

"I don't…" Jackie thought better of her words and stopped herself before she said something that she would regret. "Why didn't you let me yell at her?"

"Would it have done any good?"

Jackie pursed her lips as she thought about my question. "No."

We put our stuff in the backroom and headed back into the main area, making a few last preparations before opening the store: straightening shelves and stuff. Tammy burst into the store in a panic.

"It's raining! The display will be ruined!"

Great.

Jackie and I ran outside and grabbed anything we could. Geez, the weather turned fast, faster than I thought it would.

"Forget the hay!" I yelled at Tammy as she carried an armful of hay inside.

She dropped it on the sidewalk and reached for the candles that she had placed on the table. Cold rain hit my face, stinging it as I snatched the warmers that Tammy had placed on the display table and carted them inside. I don't know how many trips it took, but by the time we got the table inside, all three of us were soaked, and at least two of us were fuming.

Before Jackie had a chance to chew Tammy out, I opened my mouth.

"Let's get this stuff into the backroom."

"I can put..." Tammy started.

"No," I said in a firm tone. "The candles may be salvageable if we dry them off, but these warmers are ruined from the rain. We can't sell them. We are taking it all to the back room and you"—I pointed at Tammy—"are going to clean this up and dry it off. And as for the warmers, you get to explain to Mr. Stilton as to why we can't sell them now."

Tammy's eyes watered, but I didn't have time for this. We're supposed to be open, but we couldn't unlock the door until we got all this stuff out of the store area. One by one, we all picked up what we could and carried them to the backroom, dumping them in a corner. After Jackie and I hauled the display table to the back, I made Tammy sweep up any hay, feathers, and confetti that had come in as well. When she had finished, she shuffled her feet to the back to finishing cleaning. I hoped we could save the candles.

"Do you want to bring that table over here and set up the Thanksgiving display?" I asked Jackie, pointing at an unused table that was still dry.

"What about…"

"She's busy."

Jackie nodded and we carried the table to the front room, placing it where customers had to walk past it when they came inside.

"Do you need any help?" I asked her.

"No, I got it," Jackie replied.

I left her to her task and hurried over to the front door, unlocking it so that people could get in. A quick glance outside showed me that the rain had stopped. I hate this sort of weather. It would be sunny one minute and rain the next only to stop five minutes later as the sun came back out. It's enough to drive anyone crazy!

Soon after I unlocked the door, at least ten people walked in. Such a number surprised me, but this is Thanksgiving week, and a lot of people start shopping Christmas deals at this time. Though, I would assume that most would be looking for deals on electronics, not candles, unless they were just looking for the token gift that you get someone so that they won't think you forgot them, but impersonal enough to not be taken the wrong way. Oh well. It's good for business if people decided to shop here,—it helped that Mr. Stilton put an ad in the local paper—and it keeps me in a job.

I went to the cash register and waited for someone to need my assistance, while watching the customers wander around, most of whom looked to be middle-aged soccer moms searching for that token gift. Some who came in here loved candles and scented oils that can be put into our warmers, others just looked around, and the last set… token gifts.

One walked over to the new display that Jackie worked on and picked up one of the cornucopia-shaped warmers that had been placed there. Jackie smiled that irritated smile she got when people interrupted what she was doing, but she remained professional and allowed the woman to examine it. The lady put it back, but Jackie stopped her, and I watched as she explained the history of the cornucopia. The woman took it. Good 'ol Jackie. She can sell almost anything and be very persuasive, which is a plus when your job depends upon selling products.

Movement drew my attention elsewhere. I moseyed over to it, thinking that it could just be a customer searching the aisle, but it wasn't. A line of votive candles, the new Fall line, shifted just a little as though something walked over or behind it. Not knowing what else to do, I just stared at the shelf as a votive candle teetered a little before falling to the floor. A customer walked by and glanced in my direction. I smiled at him while wishing for him to go away.

Once he disappeared behind some more shelves, I turned back to the shelf of votives that seemed to be moving on its own. A few of the candles in the back tipped over as though something walked over them.

Oh no. Though I have never owned pets, I knew someone who had a cat once, and it liked to get on shelves and walk over the knick-knacks she had there. Why—why—why did he follow me here? A votive candle scooted across the shelf in micrometers, wobbling some, as though something played with it, until it fell to the floor with a plop. As I reached for it, a bang hit my ears as something jumped from a shelf to the one across from it. A package of scented wax tumbled to the floor as I dove to catch the candles. My efforts proved useless as the small packages crashed around me.

"Mew," came a soft apology above me.

I looked up and into the face of Bentley, the Russian Blue cat that had met an unfortunate end when his owner rolled her car earlier this morning. It appeared that he had decided to make himself visible, but was it only to me or everyone? I was about to find out.

Ignoring the mess on the floor, I reached up for the cat and grabbed him around the shoulders, doing my best to pull him off the shelf. His claws screeched across the metal, causing a few stares to come my way. Nervous, and not wanting the extra attention, I pulled harder, eliciting a series of meows from the cat, until I had him in my arms. Finally! I cradled the cat and did my best to stand up without dropping him when a voice I wished I never had to hear again spoke.

"Having fun?"

Jillian Mordson stood in the entrance to the aisle with her arms folded.

"What are you doing here?" I demanded, while Bentley hissed at her. Well, I guess that is one thing we both agreed on.

"Shopping," she replied.

The hell she was. "This could be called harassment, you know."

She scoffed at my statement before asking, "Is something wrong?"

Shoot! I'm still holding Bentley, but she couldn't see him, so it looked as though I was holding thin air. The cat purred as I held him, while giving her a wry smile, wondering what I should do. Knowing there was no other way to put the cat down, since I did not want to just drop him, I placed him on the floor with care before standing up with a smile, pretending that my actions were normal.

"If you're not buying anything," I said to her, "I'm going to have to ask you to leave."

"Not very customer friendly of you," mocked Jillian.

Seriously, what was her problem? Ever since I had first met her, she had done nothing but follow me around in a pathetic attempt to try and ruin my reputation. "What do you call what you're doing?"

"My job."

"What is your problem?" I tried to keep my voice down, but I had it with this woman.

Jillian put her face in front of mine and whispered, "I know you are a fraud, and one of these days, I am going to prove it."

"Again," I said to her, "if you aren't buying anything, you need to go."

Jillian grabbed a candle off a shelf and smirked at me.

Okay, have it your way, I thought to myself.

I followed her to the register and rung up her purchase. "A dollar fifty," I said to her.

"For this?" she asked, incredulous.

"I don't make the prices," I replied.

She flung six quarters on the counter and grabbed her candle.

Whatever. As I picked up the quarters, Bentley raced across the counter and knocked over an open water bottle, which I didn't even remember being there to begin with, all over Jillian, soaking her shirt and pants.

"Good kitty," I heard Rachel say, and when I turned my head, I spotted her on the other end of the counter petting Bentley. That explained where the water bottle came from.

"Why you..." Jillian began.

"You can't possibly think she had anything to do with that," Rachel said.

Jillian whirled around to see who had spoken, but she never saw Rachel, though she had heard her, so that is a change from when I had first met her. Angry, but knowing there was nothing she could do about what had just happened, she snatched her candle and stormed out the door, whipping the bell on it with such force, that I thought it would fly across the room.

"What was that all about?" Jackie whispered when she came up to me to see what she had missed.

"Just Jillian being Jillian."

"That witch," Jackie spat.

"Can I ask you a favor?"

Jackie gave me a look.

"Can you watch the register while I go clean up a mess in one of the aisles?"

"Sure. What happened?"

"Bentley and Rachel showed up," I replied.

I glanced at Rachel who dangled a string for Bentley to play with while uttering, "Who's a good kitty?"

I left Bentley with Rachel as I hurried over to the aisle where the cat had knocked down a bunch of candles, wanting to pick them up before any more customers stumbled upon them. I put them on the shelf, doing my best to organize them according to their scent. A couple of people talking in the aisle next to me grabbed my attention. It wasn't so much that they were talking, but it was what they were talking about that piqued my curiosity.

"She should not have been out driving at that time," said one.

"Who?" asked the other.

"That Paresgue woman!"

I dropped everything and leaned in closer, pushing myself against the shelves in front of me so that I could hear them better.

"Maybe she had a good reason."

"Good reason? She never went anywhere and hadn't driven in years."

"Well…"

"I just can't believe that she would risk her life like that."

Okay. I couldn't stand the suspense anymore. Why would the woman not drive at night? Wanting to know more, I did something I usually don't do when eavesdropping: I let them know what I was doing.

"Sorry," I said to one as I walked up to them, "but I couldn't help but overhear you. Are you talking about that woman that died this morning?"

"Yeah," they answered. At least they didn't seem too upset that I had been listening in.

"Why wouldn't she be driving at night?" I asked.

"Well," said one, "she had glaucoma. It was being treated and she had a license and everything, but word is, she hadn't driven in years, but instead had someone chauffer her around, except for the rare occasion when she had no choice but to drive herself. When that happened, she always made sure to do it during the day."

"Did you know her?" I asked, trying not to be too pushy, but most people don't know so much about strangers.

"Yes and no," answered the other.

My face contorted in confusion.

"You don't know?" asked the first one.

"Know what?"

"Mrs. Paresgue was an heiress. Heiress to the Paresgue fortune."

This is the problem with being an outsider. You don't know everything about the local people, especially those who can trace their origins generations back.

"They're only one of the richest people in this county. Owners of a rare blue diamond. Can't believe you know nothing about her."

I just smiled. "So, how is it you know her?"

"Well, she's kind of infirmed. She could still walk and stuff, but not very well and tired easy. Tends to happen when you reach your nineties. We volunteer with a local group that delivers meals to the elderly."

"She doesn't have any family?" I asked.

"They don't get along. I don't know the full story, but from the way she talked when we dropped off her meals, it seemed that she was estranged from them."

"And no one worked for her who could…"

"There was the chauffer, a groundskeeper, and a lady who came once a week to clean, but good help is hard to find when you're rich."

"Yeah," said the other, "stuff tends to go missing."

"She had a problem with someone stealing from her?" I asked.

"She had hired a girl a while back to cook for her and buy some groceries," replied the first one, "but some stuff had gone missing so she fired her."

"But the girl claims she never took anything."

"Not that the missing items ever stopped. Poor old woman started getting paranoid, saying that things were being moved around or disappearing."

Really? "What's the girl's name?"

"I don't know," replied the two.

"Hey, we need to go," one said to the other."

I thanked the two and wished them a good day. So, Mrs. Paresgue couldn't drive at night. Then why was she out so early in the morning, and before the sun came up. Most people aren't out that early to begin with. Where was she going?

I thought of Bentley. I don't know how he found me, but it could be that he believed his owner had some unfinished business. Either way, he's the only witness to what happened.

I rushed over to Jackie, who finished up with a customer at the cash register.

"Guess what?" I said after the customer left.

Jackie gave me a look.

"That woman who died in the car wreck this morning—she had glaucoma."

Jackie's eyebrows scrunched together.

"She couldn't drive at night."

"Then what was she doing out so early in the morning?" asked Jackie.

"It doesn't make sense. Most people aren't out at that hour, and she couldn't drive in the dark anyway. I need to see the area where she crashed."

"Are you crazy?"

"There might be a clue as to why she was out there."

"You're not going to let this go, are you?" Jackie said. She knew me too well. "After work."

"Deal."

"Got to admit," said Jackie, "I'm a little curious too."

"It wasn't an accident?" said Rachel, appearing out of nowhere like she always did. "It was murder!" she shouted with glee. She was way to giddy about this.

Heads turned in our direction and I buried my face in my hands. "Do you mind keeping it down?" I said to her.

Rachel covered her mouth with her hands and giggled. "Sorry."

She vanished, leaving Jackie and me to try and pretend that everything was normal.

Chapter 4

Jackie and I pulled up to the car sitting on the side of the road and parked. I had texted Greg before we left work, asking him if he wanted to help us look over the area where Mrs. Paresgue had crashed. Mrs. Paresgue's car had been towed away, and most of the debris cleaned up. All that remained was some bits of glass and yellow crime scene tape, probably to try and keep people away. But there were no cops around. They must have finished what they needed to do, since the entire accident is being passed off as an accident and not foul play.

Greg waved at us when we arrived. I jumped out and gave him a kiss.

"Thanks for coming," I said to him.

"So, what's this all about?" he asked.

Greg is a dear. Always willing to help me out when something won't stop bugging me, and I wasn't very specific in the text I had sent him.

"Did you read about that old lady who died this morning?" I asked.

"No."

Jackie held out her phone with the article pulled up and showed it to him. He read it before commenting, "So…"

"The cat showed up at my door this morning," I said.

Greg arched an eyebrow. He was used to Rachel's comings and goings and had been pretty open to the fact that ghosts seem to come into my life wanting me to help them with something, courtesy of Rachel, but this was the first time that a ghost cat had shown up.

"And the cat told you that the accident was no accident?" sked Greg.

I scowled at him. "Really? After everything that has happened the last few years, you're going to ask that?"

He held me closer as a way of saying he was sorry.

"Mel found some oddities to this whole incident," said Jackie.

"Such as?" asked Greg.

"The woman had glaucoma. Though she wasn't completely banned from driving because it was being treated, she didn't drive at night. It would have been pitch black out here at the time the accident occurred."

"Which begs the question: why was she out here?" said Greg. "And the cat?"

Before I could answer, something rubbed against Greg's leg, moving his pants leg a little and a tiny "merp" could be heard. Bentley must have been taking lessons from Rachel, since he appeared and disappeared at will. Or maybe it was just a cat thing.

"So, what are we looking for?" asked Greg.

"I don't know," I said.

"You don't know?" Jackie said, giving me an incredulous look. "You've got us out here in the freezing rain, and you don't know?"

"Well… I couldn't think of any other place to start. Just look for anything out of the ordinary. Anything the police might have missed."

"If Detective Shorts could see you now," joked Jackie as she wandered off, jumping over the small ditch and searched the area beyond it.

Zipping my coat up until the zipper dug into my chin, I hugged myself as I walked over to the skid marks I had spotted in the road. Misty rain coated my face, causing me to shiver even more. Geez, it's cold out here. Sometimes I don't know what was colder: snow or freezing rain. I examined the skid marks, noting how they started about… I can't even see the start of it. I follow the skid marks down the highway, growing worried as it seemed to just keep going. The farther I went, the more concerned I became. Most skid marks aren't this long. When I started to think that I wouldn't find the end, I stopped where the marks began. This was about 400 feet. How fast was she going? I've never seen skid marks that long before.

I pulled out my phone, hoping I would get a signal. Sometimes it got spotty when the weather was bad, not to mention that we were outside of the city. Good. There was a signal. I pulled up an app that would help measure the speed of a car and typed in my estimate of the skid marks. My eyes widened when the calculation of 95mph to 98mph came up. Why was she driving so fast? The speed limit was 65mph and considering the fact that it had been freezing rain early this morning, she should have slowed down for conditions. Why would an old woman with poor night vision be doing almost 100 on a lonely road in the middle of nowhere?

"Mel!" Greg called to me.

I ran over to him along with Jackie.

Greg handed me a thin, black pouch.

I took it, noting that the flap was open and the contents were missing.

"What is it?" asked Jackie.

"Not sure," I said.

"I found it here. Look, there's a small booklet." Greg pickup it up and held it out to me. "It looks like a manual to a car."

I took the booklet and placed it in the small pouch. It fit.

"Could it have belonged to the old lady's car?" asked Jackie.

"It's possible," I said. "Depending on how bad the accident was, it could have been flung from the car as the windows broke."

"Considering the old lady and her cat died, I'd say it was a bad accident," said Jackie.

"Yes… that's not what I meant," I said.

"Find anything else?" asked Greg.

"Those skid marks are about 400 feet in length," I replied.

Jackie whistled. "How fast was she going?"

"Almost 98mph," I said.

Both Greg and Jackie gave me a long look and I held up my phone, showing them the app I had used to calculate the speed.

"What was she in a hurry to get to?" asked Jackie.

"Or running away from?" said Greg.

Good questions, and I had no answers to either of them.

"Are we almost done here?" asked Jackie. "Cuz I'm freezing."

I agreed. The rain continued to come down, soaking my coat, and each drop was like a pinprick of cold that zipped through my skin and to my bones. I shivered.

"Meow."

I turned in the direction of the meow and saw Bentley sitting next to a bush, staring at me as though I should have already known what he wanted and what he sat next to. I wandered over to him as he sat all regal like, as though he owned this desolate place. His paw rested on a torn piece of paper. I picked it up, trying to be careful, since it was soaked, and I didn't want to tear it or cause it to disintegrate. Bentley purred as I picked up the paper. I looked at it closer, while the cat wove a figure eight between my legs. I could make out the name Paresgue and a partial address, but that was it.

Before I could head back to Jackie and Greg, Bentley meowed and ran off, stopping by a rock. At first, I thought he was just being a cat, and didn't think to follow him, until he released a series of insistent meows, forcing me to look at what he wanted. Holding the wet paper scrap with care, I walked over to Bentley, not liking the way my shoes stuck to the mud worse than glue does to paper. The cat pawed at something on the ground that was covered in mud. I picked it up, wiping the slimy gunk off of it. It was a cat collar, but not some run-of-the-mill collar that can be bought in any major pet store; this was fancy, as in, it probably cost a few hundred dollars fancy.

"Was this yours?" I asked Bentley.

He purred in response and rubbed against my legs, and even though he was a spirit, I still felt the pressure against my skin as he butted against them.

I read somewhere that ghosts tend to appear as they did in life. When I had first met Bentley, he was wearing a collar—and I hadn't realized he wasn't a spirit—but that was because he probably always wore the collar when he was alive, but it is just a manifestation, if that makes sense. Somehow, his real collar ended up in the mud here.

"Is this where you died?" I asked the cat, feeling bad for him.

Bentley's ears drooped a little and he ran off with his tail low, and the sense that I had brought up a bad memory filled me.

I checked the collar in my hand, rubbing some more mud off it and noticed that the clasp had broken. This was why it was buried in the mud. Even if the EMTs had picked up the cat's body, they wouldn't be looking for his collar. But why would Bentley want me to find it? Maybe he was attached to it and wanted it back.

Rain dripped down the back of my neck, causing me to shiver and I hurried back to Jackie and Greg.

"Here," I handed the paper scrap to Greg. "This could be her address."

Greg took it, but it was difficult to make out the full address.

"We need that address."

"Why? You want to break into her house?" asked Jackie. She didn't need to see my face to know the answer. "Of course, you do. Well, we can look it up on the web. She was rich, right? We should be able to…"

"It won't work," interrupted Greg.

"What?" Jackie and I said together.

"She had a P.O. address that she used for all her mail, including her insurance and license. She kept her home address private. She didn't want people to just show up at her place and harass her."

"Why would anyone do that?" I asked.

"Do you not pay attention to the news?" asked Jackie. "There are groups of people that make a profession out of harassing others whom they view as wealthy and un-deserving. Honestly, if I were some ninety-year-old lady living alone, I wouldn't want my address or number pub-licized because we live in a crazy world."

"No argument there," I said.

"And how did you discover all this?" Jackie asked Greg.

"Jack," said Greg. "I called him while you two were looking around."

"And what did he say?" asked Jackie.

"Pretty much what I told you before hanging up on me."

"I guess we'll have to go see him," I said.

"Uh… no," said Jackie. "We are going home where I am taking a hot shower and getting some hot chocolate."

It was cold, and my hair had turned into a waterfall because of all the rain. "I can always go, if you want to…"

"No," interrupted Jackie. "By we, I meant you."

I leaned in to kiss Greg when Jackie grabbed my arm and dragged me away.

"Come on," she said, forcing me to the car.

"Can't I say good-bye to my boyfriend?" I asked as Greg tried to not laugh at my plight.

"You'll see him tomorrow."

Jackie shoved me into the passenger seat of the car and shut the door, before getting in herself.

"A little bossy, aren't you?" I said.

"It's cold and I'm wet." She started the car and drove away, forcing me to wave at Greg with a sheepish smile, while he still laughed at her forcefulness.

I didn't see any sign of Bentley. Guess he showed me what he wanted me to see. And Rachel? Who knew where she was? She was always someplace, and where that was depended upon her current mood.

Chapter 5

Jackie and I walked through the door to our apartment and stopped the moment we turned the lights on and saw what awaited us inside. Next to the window by the TV was a cat tree, but not just any cat tree, this one had five levels, with a padded, broad shelf at the very top, perfect for any cat to lay on. Feathers dangled from the other shelves in such a way to entice any feline to play with it; and if that didn't interest them, the tree had a tunnel for kitties to hide in. I just stared at it as it stretched up to the ceiling, wondering how it got here and what I was to do with it.

Both Jackie and I stepped inside and stopped the moment our feet stepped on some squishy cat toys. Toy mice and furry balls littered the apartment floor along with a collapsible tube.

Jackie looked around the room, threw up her hands, saying, "She's your problem."

Rachel. How else would all of this stuff end up in the apartment? Oh, my God! What if one of my neighbors saw her? I don't need them thinking that they live in a haunted building, or that I am the cause of it all. As though people don't already think I am a little odd, let's just add a ghost shopping for me and carrying all this stuff in here. Wait a minute? How did she pay for it?

"Hey, Mel!"

I ran to the kitchen when I heard Jackie calling my name and almost fainted when I saw a fountain stretching from the tile floor to the top of the counter top with three levels, each with intricate designs of cats playing, and all three of which had water flowing from one to the other.

"What the…" I began.

Rachel popped in to the room. "Do you like it?"

"Like it?" I said. "What is all this stuff doing here?"

Rachel held her hands behind her back and shuffled her feet. "Well, Bentley needs something to make his own."

Really? She bought all of this for a dead cat? I felt bad for it dying in a horrific car crash, but he was still just a spirit. "Rachel, Bentley is dead," I said, trying not to sound rude, but I failed.

"That's insensitive, you know," said Rachel.

"Right," Jackie piped in, "while you two hash this out, I'm going to go take a hot shower." She walked off, and I listened as she went into the bathroom and the water turned on. Taking a hot bath sounded good right about now, but it would have to wait.

I remembered that we had never shut the front door and hurried over to it. "I understand you are trying to help him," I said to Rachel as I hurried to the door, "but you have to know that Bentley isn't going to stick around here for long? Isn't there a place animals go to when they die?"

"I assume they go where their people go," said Rachel.

"What am I to do with all this stuff?" I asked.

"Keep it and get a cat."

I gave her a look. "How did you pay for all this?"

Rachel looked away.

"Rachel?" This wouldn't be the first time she borrowed my money to buy stuff, but this was going overboard.

"Now, don't get mad."

My heart sank. Anytime someone used those words, it meant I was going to blow a gasket, or something. "Rachel, how did you pay for all this?"

"Promise you won't get mad?"

I grounded my teeth, wondering if I should make such a promise as the gnawing feeling that I would not like her answer ate at me.

"Your credit card," she said with a grin.

My face must have gone purple because she jumped back and blurted out, "You promised!"

I inhaled deeply, held my breath, and exhaled in a long, slow fashion, trying to calm myself. "I do remember telling you to quit borrowing my wallet for purchases."

"I know," Rachel replied, giving me an innocent look.

Okay. Not getting mad. I'm just a little peeved. "How much?" I asked.

"What?"

Jack's help to determine what it said. I just hoped that it wasn't too ruined by the rain. I turned the water off once I finished washing, and dried off. A message in the fog in the mirror stopped me for a moment.

"Sorry," it read.

I shook my head and chuckled a little, knowing that the message came from Rachel, though it was a little weird that she snuck into the bathroom just to leave an apology note. Sometimes she was so aggravating that I could kill her, if she wasn't dead already. I hurried to my room and put some clothes before going to the kitchen for some hot chocolate. Jackie had beat me to it already.

"On the counter," Jackie said from the couch, having already curled up under a blanket with her own cup of hot cocoa while watching a show on Hulu.

I grabbed the cup that had been set aside for me, grabbed the scrap of paper and collar that I had set on the table by the door, and sat down on the couch next to Jackie.

"What are you watching?" I asked.

"Finishing up *The Handmaid's Tale*," she replied. "You should watch it."

"Maybe later." I twirled the collar in my fingers while staring at the scrap of paper and the partial address on it. There had to be a reason as to why Bentley wanted me to find these. Greg won't be home for a while, so I can't talk to him about it. But maybe Jack could help me, though he is a tough nut to crack.

Jack and Greg are cousins, and Greg usually used innocent blackmail to get Jack to help us out when we needed information regarding a mystery I was involved in. Nothing serious. Apparently, they grew up together and Jack did some stupid stuff that he doesn't want the rest of his family to know about, except Greg knew, and sometimes threatened, to tell on him if he didn't help.

A knock sounded at the door.

"Who could that be?" asked Jackie, pausing her show.

I shook my head and went to the door, hoping that my neighbor didn't call the cops on me for yelling at what must have looked like thin air to her. That was just what I didn't need: trying to explain to the police why I was yelling at a ghost earlier.

I opened the door to find Tiny standing there. This was unexpected. He looked upset, which was unusual for him.

"Hey, Mel."

"What's wrong?" I asked, letting him in.

"I think Elise has left me."

"What?" Jackie almost jumped over the back of the couch at this news.

"What happened?" I asked.

"We were out shopping so that she could get some new pants, and when she tried some on, she asked me what I thought."

"You told her she looked great, right?" asked Jackie.

"I told her the truth," Tiny said.

"You told her she looked great," Jackie reiterated.

Tiny looked around, wringing his hands as he thought about what to say. It's a bit odd for a big man like Tiny to seem so out of sorts and to be afraid of speaking, but whatever it was he did say to his girlfriend, it couldn't have been good.

"I told her that she might want to consider going up a size," he said.

Jackie and I both cringed.

"You never want to say that to a woman," Jackie said.

"But it was the truth," replied Tiny. "She didn't look comfortable, and… well… she has put on some weight within the last year."

"She's not…" I began.

"No," Tiny said. "She can't get pregnant. An accident from her childhood took that ability away."

I never knew that. I've known Tiny and Elise for a few years now and never knew that she suffered an accident that made it where she couldn't have kids.

"Seriously?" said Jackie, intrigued, but concerned.

"We don't publicize it," said Tiny.

I went to the kitchen and made a cup of hot chocolate and gave it to Tiny, encouraging him to sit down. "Weight gain can happen to all of us, but you never suggest that your girlfriend should go up a size."

"Why?" asked Tiny.

"That's like calling her fat," said Jackie. "At least, that is how she sees it. You hurt her feelings."

"She won't talk to me," moaned Tiny.

"She'll forgive you," I said. "Just say you're sorry and give her time."

"Take her to her favorite place to eat for a romantic dinner. Get her flowers and candy, or beer and brass knuckles in her case. Seems to be more up her alley. I know a place that is still open," said Jackie.

"Are you two trying to get rid of me?" Tiny asked, and even I had the feeling that Jackie was trying to do just that.

"Mel has a new mystery she needs to solve and won't stop talking about it until she has, and while you're here, she can't do that. I'm trying to finish a show. So, the sooner I solve your problem, the sooner Mel can fix hers, and the sooner I can finish my show."

"Hulu isn't going anywhere anytime soon," I chided her as I went to the kitchen and grabbed a cup of hot cocoa for Tiny.

"You never know," replied Jackie. "Disney might buy them out."

"They already have," I whispered to her.

"Really?" said Jackie. "Sheesh."

"Mystery? And did you get a cat or something?" Tiny asked, noticing all the cat stuff for the first time.

"That would be Mel's new mystery," Jackie said.

Tiny arched an eyebrow.

"An old lady died, her cat showed up, and Rachel has taken it upon herself to buy out the pet store," I replied.

"What sort of mystery?" asked Tiny.

"The Mrs. Paresgue woman," I said.

"Are you kidding me?" Tiny blurted out. "You think she was murdered?"

"I don't know," I replied, "but she was out driving in the wee hours of the morning and wasn't supposed to be driving at night. It's just odd. Why was she out so early when she could have waited for morning and called a cab?"

"Fair point," said Tiny.

"And her cat showed up and has been leading me from one clue to the next," I said.

"Such as?" asked Tiny.

"Such as this." I held up the scrap of paper. "I was about to call Jack and see if he could help me figure out if this is an actual address."

"Call away." Tiny leaned back in his chair gulping his hot chocolate.

I grabbed my phone and dialed Jack's number putting it on speaker. He answered on the second ring.

"What?"

Always so cheerful. "Jack, I need your help."

"No."

"But…"

"No," said Jack. "No more. Neither you, my cousin, or that big, dumb oaf of yours will convince me to help you."

Tiny's fingers tightened as Jack hung up. "Give me the phone," he said.

Tiny redialed Jack's number and waited for the call to connect.

"Look, Mel…" came Jack's voice.

"This is the big, dumb oaf," Tiny growled into the phone.

Jack went silent, and I imagined all the curse words going through his mind at that moment.

"Look, man, I didn't…"

"Silence," said Tiny. He took my phone off speaker, got up, and went into the other room. "Now listen good," I heard him say as he walked away.

"What do you think he is saying to him?" whispered Jackie.

"Probably how he is going to tear him from limb to limb," I whispered back.

I didn't know how many minutes had passed before Tiny came back into the room and put my phone on speaker.

"Now, tell her what you found out," Tiny told Jack.

"Like I told your boyfriend," Jack began, "Mrs. Paresgue had two addresses. She used one which belonged to a small residence in the city for her mail, identification cards, and her main bills. That is the address on the piece of the insurance card that you have."

Jack read the address, and I wrote it down.

"So, she had a second address," said Jackie.

"Yes," replied Jack. "This is where she lived. Only those closest to her knew about all this and were sworn to secrecy, I guess. It took a little digging, but I managed to find it."

"How?" I asked.

"There is always a paper trail somewhere, no matter how small. The home was registered under a different name, but every building will experience power and water usage if someone is living there, which means they will have bills."

"How'd you learn all this?"

"I had to get a little creative," replied Jack.

I didn't want to know what Jack had to do to find this all out.

"She is part of one of the oldest families in the county, right?" asked Jackie. "How is it she managed to keep such a low profile?"

"Most people knew about her brother and her husband," replied Jack, "not her. She never went out much. Stayed to herself. She never did anything to bring attention to herself. Also, the family home had been sold over ten years ago to pay off some debts and she seemed to have had enough left over to purchase two residences: one for living in, and one for the public to know about."

"Where is it?" I asked.

"I don't know..." began Jack.

Tiny glowered at the phone, and Jack changed his mind, almost as though he saw Tiny's change in facial expressions. I really wanted to know what he had said to Jack to get him to change his mind about helping me.

Jack read off the second address and I wrote it down.

"Thanks, Jack," I said.

"Yeah, you're welcome," he mumbled. "And you're not going to back out?" he said to Tiny.

"I said I'd be there," Tiny growled into the phone before hanging up and handing me my phone back.

I stared at the two addresses that I had written down, thinking that there had to be a reason as to why Bentley had shown me the scrap of insurance paper. Maybe he wants me to go to these residences. But which one do I go to first? I decided on the second one I had written down, the one where the old woman lived. If there was anything to be found, it's most likely in the house that she lived in, not the one she kept around for receiving mail.

"I know that look," Jackie said.

"What look?" I asked, trying to sound innocent.

"That look you get every time you're about to do something crazy."

"I'm not going to do anything crazy," I said before turning to Jackie. "Just go back to your show."

I faced Tiny. "And go apologize to Elise. Take her

somewhere special. I'm sure she'll forgive you. And the next time she asks about an outfit, tell her that she is beautiful no matter what."

I headed for my room.

"Where are you going?" asked Jackie.

"Just going to wait until Greg gets home," I replied.

Tiny stopped me. Darn it! They knew me too well.

"You're going there, aren't you?" said Jackie.

"I'm…"

"All right. I'll be dressed in a few." She pushed herself off the couch and went to her room, exiting a few minutes later all dressed in skinny jeans, a square-necked, empire waist blouse, and an elegant white, winter coat. I always marveled at how Jackie always looked picture perfect and put together, while I usually looked like I had just crawled out of bed. I'm getting better with my wardrobe choices, thanks to Jackie's help, but I have a long way to go.

"Come on," said Jackie, grabbing her keys and phone and heading for the door. "Time's a wasting."

I grabbed a coat, which already had a tear in the side, shoved my phone and keys in my pocket and followed after Jackie.

Tiny clearing his throat, stopping us. I had forgotten he was still here. "Just where do you two think you are going?"

"I thought we had made that clear," quipped Jackie. "We're going to break into some dead, old lady's home."

"In the middle of the night?" said Tiny.

"No time like the present," replied Jackie, growing impatient.

"You expect me to let the both of you go break into someone's home in the middle of the night?"

"Yeah," said Jackie.

"You ain't going," said Tiny.

Jackie put her hands on her hips, looking like she wanted to tackle him, which would be quite a site, when Tiny spoke again.

"Unless I come with you."

"What?" Jackie's face went from being ready to kill someone to being confused, while I tried to stop from laughing, remembering that Tiny loved bending the law a few times, and the few times he had helped me do something slightly illegal.

"You're going to break into someone's home to figure out why she was out on such a terrible night, and you think I'm not coming?"

He headed for the door and opened it for us.

"You got another think coming," he said, waving Jackie and me through the door.

Chapter 6

I parked the car down the road from the estate and near some bushes, away from the front gate and prying eyes. I didn't need someone to spot us and call the police, since I had no idea how I would explain this to Detective Shorts. He was getting to know me pretty well. Tiny shifted in the back seat as I turned off the engine. He didn't like having to ride back there, but I had pointed out that his motorcycle might make too much noise, and we were trying to go incognito.

"I should text Greg," I said, before getting out of the car.

"You're just now thinking of that?" asked Jackie.

"You didn't exactly remind me," I replied.

"True," Jackie said.

Tiny opened his door. "I already took care of it."

"What?" I snatched his phone from his hand and looked at the last message he had sent.

"Seriously?" I said, incredulous. "You told him that I was going to break into someone's house, but promised not to steal anything, and that he shouldn't worry because you're here and we're only 'slightly breaking the law'?"

"It's true," Tiny replied.

"You probably should have worded it differently," Jackie added. "Now, come on. The longer we're here, the better chance we have of getting caught."

No argument there.

We got out of the car and hiked across the road to the metal fence, with spiked posts, that went around the Mrs. Paresgue's property. We hunkered behind some bushes and looked through the fence posts, wondering how we were going to climb over it, since none of us wanted to get poked by the spikes. Only a few lights were on in the house, but I didn't see anyone wandering around. I wondered if some lights were left on just to make it look like someone was home.

"How are we going to get through this fence?" Jackie asked.

Good question. Before I could say anything, Tiny found a solution. He tossed his jacket onto the spikes, covering them and motioned for Jackie to come to him as he cupped his hands. Knowing what he planned, Jackie placed her foot in his cupped hands and he hoisted her over the fence, while his jacket provided a barrier between her and the spikes, and she landed on the other side with grace and ease. Tiny hissed my name. Well, here I go. I placed my right foot in his hands and he lifted me over the fence, but my hand slipped as I grabbed the bars, which shifted the jacket and allowed one of the spikes to put another tear in my coat. I landed on my side with a thump. So much for being graceful.

"You okay?" Jackie asked me.

"Yeah," I replied, checking the newly formed rip in my coat. Guess I'll have to buy a new one at some point. Ugh. I hate shopping.

Tiny's boots made soft thuds on the grass next to me as he hopped over the fence and grabbed his jacket, putting it back on. He waved us over to some more bushes, urging us to hide.

"Do you see anyone?" I asked.

"No," replied Tiny.

"I wonder how we are to get in there," said Jackie. "A place like this has to have an alarm system."

Crap! I didn't think about that. Even Tiny seemed a little worried about that.

"Meow."

I turned my head. Bentley sat in the middle of the yard just staring at me as though I was an idiot and should have known what he knew.

"Meow," he said again and darted off.

"Bentley!" I called after him, though I tried to keep my voice low so as not to attract attention.

"Mel!" Jackie ran after me with Tiny close behind.

We ran across the wet grass, leaving a mangled mess of footprints, as I chased after Bentley, wondering where he was taking me, while Tiny and Jackie followed. Once I reached the back door, I stopped. There was no sign of Bentley. Where did he go? Panicked that I had lost him, I searched around the patio, checking under the chairs and table, thinking that I had just chased after the spirit of a cat for nothing.

"Mel," Jackie breathed as she ran up beside me.

"Bentley was here," I said.

"What?"

"I saw him."

"Mel, we're too exposed here," Jackie said.

She was right. I hurried to the side of the house, joining Tiny as he checked some windows, but stopped when I heard another meow. I turned just in time to see Bentley's tail disappear through the back door. What?

I hurried over to the door, ready to give that cat a piece of my mind. Did he think we could just go through solid objects? I knew Rachel sometimes did.

Tiny chased after me. "Mel, what did I teach you about sneaking into someone's house?"

"I saw him go through here," I whispered.

"Who?" asked Tiny.

"Bentley. The old lady's cat."

Tiny gave me a doubtful look, but I ignored him as I felt the door where I had seen the cat go, knocking on it just a little. The sounds change. I hit the area the cat had gone through before tapping another part of the door, confirming the change of tone.

"Listen," I said, tapping the door again.

Tiny heard the change in sound and pushed me aside as he inspected the door more closely. "There's a pet door here," he said, "but it's disguised to look just like this door. Probably so no one knows what it is or that it is here."

He pushed against it, but it refused to open.

"Why show us to a door that is locked?" asked Jackie, looking around to make sure that no one had spotted us.

"It might be one of those that requires your pet to wear a special collar for it to open."

The collar. I pulled the collar I had found on the side of the road earlier, glad that I had thought to put it in my pocket, and placed it near the pet door. Something clicked and Tiny pushed it inward. It wasn't a cat-sized door, but seemed to be big enough for a medium-sized dog.

"I wonder if any of us can fit through," I said.

"Don't look at me," replied Tiny.

I chuckled a little, remembering the time I had to help him crawl through a window because he had gotten stuck. I did not need that again. My eyes settled on Jackie who pretended that she wasn't listening.

"What?" she said to me.

"You're skinny," I said.

"So, are you," she snapped.

"But not as thin as you," I replied, "and you're more agile."

She glared at me, and I knew what she thought: she didn't want her white coat to get dirty, not that I blamed her, but it was cold out here, and either we got inside and looked around, or left and admitted that this entire trip was a waste.

"Fine," said Jackie.

She got down on her hands and knees and crawled to the door, while Tiny held it open. It was smaller than we had thought, forcing Jackie to get on her stomach and inch her way through like a worm.

"Oh, I knew I should have worn a different coat," she said.

She stopped.

"Keep going," I urged her.

"I'm stuck," Jackie said.

This wasn't good.

"Are you sure?" I asked.

"Do you honestly think I would lie about such a thing when I am halfway through a dog door, while trying to sneak into some stranger's house in the middle of the night when it is this cold outside?"

The sarcasm in Jackie's voice told me that I needed to think of something quick. I tried to push her through, but her rump was thoroughly stuck, and neither Tiny, nor I, knew what to do.

"Help me," pleaded Jackie. The only thing I could think of was to either pull her out, but I really needed to get inside, or Tiny and I would have to both push her through at the same time.

"Grab a leg," I told Tiny.

He did.

"When I say, push."

Tiny nodded.

"What? Wait!" Jackie's voice came through the door, but I ignored her. We had to get her out of the pet door.

"Now!" I said to Tiny.

We both pushed as hard as we could, and I felt Jackie go through the door, while at the same time, a loud rip filled the air, making me dread its meaning. With her butt freed from the pet door's hold on her, Jackie wriggled the rest of the way inside and swore a little once she stood up. I knew what had torn, and it wouldn't be pretty.

The door opened and Jackie stood there, glaring at me, while holding a flap of material that had now hung at an odd angle from the rest of her coat.

"I'll buy you a new one," I promised.

"Oh, I know you will," said Jackie, "but this isn't what has me so steamed." She turned around so that I could see the back end of her jeans, and the hole that was now in them, allowing the world the ability to glimpse her festive, confetti printed underwear.

"And I'll buy you some new jeans," I said in a meek voice, hoping she wouldn't kill me.

Tiny broke up our banter and urged us to get inside, closing the door and making no noise.

"And don't you dare look," Jackie rounded on Tiny before walking through the kitchen and into the dining room.

"Wasn't gonna," whispered Tiny, trying not to laugh.

"I heard that chuckle," Jackie said.

Tiny shushed us and I followed her into the dining room, almost stopping when I saw the long table with a velvet table cloth covering its mahogany surface. A vase with fresh flowers sat in the center, and despite the gloomy night, their bright colors reflected what light could touch them. I ran my fingers along the petals, assuring myself that they were real and not fake. Not sure what I would find in the dining room, I moved into a sitting room, almost tripping over the leg of an ornate chair with blue cushions on it. The old-fashioned looking chair made me wonder if all of the furniture in this place was old or made to look old. The soft cushions indicted that they weren't used as much, since there were no permanent impressions in them and the stuffing hadn't been squished down, but they had no dust on them either, meaning that someone cleaned them on a regular basis.

The end tables in the room were evenly spaced apart and each had a covering draping over the sides with books situated in a neat pile on them. I picked one up: *The Count of Monte Cristo*. Not exactly light reading. I wondered if Mrs. Paresgue actually read these books or if they were more for decoration. Bentley meowed again, drawing my attention toward a painting in the other room. Putting the book down, I moseyed to the painting, taking out my phone and turning on its flashlight, shining the beam on the painting. A woman, wearing a small blue diamond necklace—it was so small that I almost missed it—and who looked to be in her eighties and holding a Russian blue cat, that looked a lot like Bentley, filled the canvas. I took a closer look, and it was Bentley in the painting with the old woman, but he looked a little younger in it, making me wonder how old he was. Focusing my beam of light on the cat in the painting, I noticed the collar he wore; it looked just like the one I had seen on Bentley the night he first appeared at my apartment, and it matched the collar I had found at the scene of the accident. I pulled he collar out of my pocket and placed it on the canvas next to the one pictured in the painting, still wondering why someone would buy such a fancy thing for their pet to wear. Come on, I reminded myself, people buy their pets fancy stuff all the time. A quick sweep of the room showed more pictures of the cat, and it became clear to me that Mrs. Paresgue's only joy in life was her cat.

"Have you guys found anything?" I whispered.

"Not really," replied Jackie.

"Just a lot of photos of some cat," said Tiny as he picked up a picture frame with another photo of Bentley. "I'm not sure what you hope to find here, Mel."

Neither am I. I had hoped something would stand out, but all of these photos show nothing that might cause Mrs. Paresgue to leave her house on such a terrible night.

"Meow!"

I flung my flashlight beam to the source of the meow and saw Bentley sitting on the bottom step of a staircase that led to the second floor.

"What is it, Bentley?" I asked, wondering what he wanted.

The cat ran up the stairs and disappeared.

Maybe he wanted me to follow him. "Hey, guys," I called, though doing my best to keep my voice low, "over here."

"Did you find something," asked Jackie.

"No," I replied, "but I think Bentley wants us to go upstairs."

Jackie frowned a little, but she didn't question me. Over the last few years, she has learned to tolerate the fact that spirits show up every so often, asking for my help in solving the mystery of how they died, or helping me in the process. This was just the first time that some-one's pet had chosen to appear. I followed after the furry animal, wondering what he wanted me to see. I crept up the carpeted stairs, hoping that there wasn't that one step that always creaked whenever someone stepped on it and breathed a sigh of relief when I reached the top without making any noise. Jackie and Tiny were right behind me.

Another sitting room was at the other end of the stairwell with five chairs forming a circle around a coffee table, but on the other end of the room was a desk. I swept the room with my flashlight and just as the beam passed over the desk, a pen fell to the floor as though it had been pushed off by something. I headed for it.

"More pictures of her cat," Jackie said, picking up another framed photo of Bentley. "This gives crazy cat lady a whole new meaning."

"Be glad she only had the one," laughed Tiny. "Ow!"

I whirled around to face him, my face puzzled from his outburst.

"Something scratched me," said Tiny.

I noticed a tail disappear around the leg of a chair and into the shadows. "I think you angered Bentley," I said.

Tiny stopped, his face a mixture of anxiety and confusion. "Sorry," he muttered.

Bentley ignored him and walked back to the desk, jumping on it and knocking something else to the floor. I hurried over there and picked it up, noting that it was a notepad, but that there were impressions in the paper. I found a pencil and swiped it across the paper until I had coated the entire thing, revealing the writing that had been done on the previous page, and a message, but it was garbled and incoherent.

"Look at this," I said, holding out the paper.

Tiny took it. "…need to… in… don't trust… now…" He looked at me. "What does all this mean?"

Jackie took the paper and studied it, noting the strip that bound the pad together. "It looks like someone has torn a bunch of paper off this pad. That's why the message is jumbled. You're getting the impressions that a pen had made several pieces of paper down from the original."

"Why would someone tear all of those pages off?" I asked.

"To hide something," said Tiny.

"None of this makes any sense," I said. "We still have no idea why Mrs. Paresgue was out one such a night."

A soft banging sound escaped from the desk as though something was trying to open the built-in cabinet. A small meow told me that Bentley made the noise, but why? I opened the small cabinet and a bunch of paper fell onto the desk, scattering everywhere. Picking one up, I studied it, realizing that it is an authentication document, dated just a few years ago, and attached to it was an image of a blue diamond. I handed it to Tiny who looked at it before giving it to Jackie.

"This diamond seems familiar," said Jackie.

"Familiar how?" I asked.

"I don't know, but…"

Before she could finish, the front door opened and a woman walked inside, turning on a single lamp. We all hid. I jumped behind a chair, and Jackie dived under the desk, while Tiny hugged the wall, staying out of the light. Peeking around the chair and through the banister, I watched as the woman marched across the front room and toward the stairs, her heels clicking on the tile floor with each purposeful step. She tore her hat off her head and swung it back and forth as she moved. I didn't know who she was, but her entire demeanor indicated that she was angry.

I motioned for Tiny and Jackie to follow me when the woman reached the bottom step. Staying low, we rushed form the upper loft to a room I had spotted moments before. I closed the door behind us, leaving it open just enough to peek through, just as the woman reached the top step. She paused for a moment before hurrying to the desk, ripping open the drawers and the cabinet, rifling through the papers in there, though she seemed to be favoring her arm. She acted like a madwoman as she searched for something.

My phone rang.

Shoot!

My fingers fumbled as I rushed to turn it off and hit the hang up button. It was Greg, no doubt wanting to know about the text message that Tiny had sent him earlier. We all jumped away from the door and flung ourselves against the wall when the woman looked in our direction. I hoped she hadn't seen me, but before she could take a step in my direction, the overhead light in the upper loft turned on, stopping her.

"What are you doing here?" demanded a man's voice.

"I don't have to answer to you," snapped the woman.

She searched through the papers some more, until she found what she wanted and clutched it in her fist. She started to walk, but the man stopped her.

"You know you're not invited here," he said.

She jerked her arm from his grip. "My aunt's dead. You work for me now." Clutching the paper she had come for, the woman headed straight for us. I hit Tiny on the chest, signaling to him that we needed to get out.

He ran to the window and looked out, examining the jump we would have to make before waving Jackie and me over. I locked the door to the room before hurrying to the window. Jackie had already gone out the window.

I paused when I reached it and realized what Tiny wanted me to do. "Are you kidding me?" I whispered.

Right outside the window was a trellis that was not attached to the building, and I couldn't believe what it was I was about to do.

"Just jump on the trellis and climb down," Tiny said.

The door rattled as the person on the other side tried to open it, growing angrier by the second.

Heart pounding, and somewhat glad Rachel wasn't here to see me, I sat on the windowsill and swung my feet outside, focusing on the trellis before jumping. It shook underneath my weight as I landed on it, and my left foot poked through one of the holes, causing the wood to scrap my thigh. Clinging to the trellis, I pulled my leg out and crawled across the top to the side. Jackie had already reached the ground. I reached the edge of the trellis and eased my way downward, until I was just a few feet from the ground, when I let go and landed on the soft grass.

Soon after I hopped off the trellis, Tiny jumped, causing it to sway side to side, and for a moment, I thought it was going to collapse. Jackie and I watched in anxious anticipation as he wormed his was to the edge and shimmied down to the ground. We both let our breaths out when his feet touched the grass.

"Let's get out of here," Jackie said.

Tiny and I agreed. We all turned around and stopped when we saw a rifle pointed right at us.

"What are you all doing here?" demanded the man holding the rifle, and I recognized his voice as the same man who had been talking to the woman earlier.

"Um…" I began.

I noticed a wisp of hair from the window we had all escaped from as the woman disappeared.

"Answer me!" yelled the man.

"I… I… I really don't have an answer," I said.

"Hey, man," said Tiny, "why don't you put that down?"

"Okay, don't answer me," said the man. "I've already called the cops."

The squeal of tires as a car pulled away attracted all of our attention, and the man with the weapon cussed as it pulled away. The woman must have run off.

There was nothing for us to do but stand in the cold, in the wet grass, and wait for the police to show, which didn't take long. I lowered my head when Detective Shorts stepped out of one of the cars. I was wondering when I was going to run into him.

Detective Shorts looked at me and grimaced, though he didn't seem that surprised to see me. By now he should be used to me being where I shouldn't be.

"Miss Summers," said Detective Shorts, and I could tell by the tone of his voice that he was not pleased to find me here, not that I could blame him; I did break into someone's house, but in my defense, she was dead.

"Why, hello, detective," greeted Jackie in a jovial tone, and both Tiny and I stared at her, wondering if she had somehow managed to get into the wine cooler, "fancy meeting you here."

"Jackie," said the detective. He looked at Tiny and released a long sigh. "I'm not surprised to see you here."

"I should be insulted by that," said Tiny. Tiny and his friends tended to live outside the law a little, nothing to big, but they were known for bending the rules a little.

"What are you three doing here?" asked Detective Shorts.

"I want them prosecuted," said the groundskeeper.

"Hold on a minute," said the detective, holding up his hand and before the officers with him could put us into handcuffs. He looked at me, somehow knowing that I was the instigator, not that he was wrong. "What are you doing you here?"

Before I could answer, the groundskeeper interjected.

"They were trespassing. Probably broke into the house and took something."

"Please," Detective shorts stopped the man. "I want to hear it from them."

"He's not wrong," I said, "except about the stealing part. We didn't take anything."

"How do I know you didn't?" challenged the groundskeeper.

Tiny growled in response and looked like he was ready to tackle the guy, but stopped when Detective Shorts screamed, "Enough, all of you!"

"Now," Detective Shorts began again, "I want to hear from them, and only them, why they are here."

The groundskeeper clamped his mouth shut, incensed at being told to shut up, but the detective wasn't playing around either, and something told me that he had something important he was doing before he got interrupted by all of this.

"I read the article about Mrs. Paresgue dying in a car accident early this morning," I said.

"And that brings you out here because…" prompted Detective Shorts.

I looked at the groundskeeper before answering the detective's unfinished question. "I don't think it was an accident."

The groundskeeper started to open his mouth, but the detective stopped him.

"And what brought you to this conclusion?"

"You know Mel," interrupted Jackie. "A person dies, it must be murder. Either way, she's not going to stop until she finds out the truth."

"And is that why you two are out here?" asked the detective.

"Can't let her have all the fun," said Jackie. "Why would anyone want to stay home on a night like this?"

"And you?" the detective asked Tiny.

"Wouldn't miss this for the world," Tiny replied in a flat tone.

"Mel." Detective Shorts waved me over to the side to speak with me privately, knowing that I did not want to say the real reason why I was here. "What is going on? Mrs. Paresgue's death was an automobile accident."

"Tell that to her cat," I said.

"Her cat? Her cat was found at the scene—deceased."

"I know." I waited a few seconds before continuing. "And he showed up at my apartment this morning."

"He showed up… Miss Summers, I know that you…"

"Yeah, you do," I said. "That's why you asked me to help a while back when that guy died in a clock."

Detective Shorts was in a precarious situation. He didn't want to admit that ghosts tended to show up once in a while, yet he couldn't deny the time the three girls followed him home, or the time Rachel decided to make her presence known when he got sent to the hospital.

"I'm sorry," I said, "but her cat did show up and seems to think that there is more to Mrs. Paresgue's death than we know."

Detective Shorts took a deep breath and was about to say something when a cat screeched and knocked over a garbage can. I spotted Bentley darting around a corner, though I don't think anyone else saw him. The tumbling trash can clattered as it crashed onto the ground and its lid popped off, allowing its contents to spill, but it was what spilled out that caught our attention. Clothes, not modern ones, but styles that were new decades ago, littered the grass, and one blouse in particular had what looked like blood on it. The groundskeeper walked over to it and reached for it, but stopped when Detective Shorts yelled at him.

"Get an evidence bag," the detective said to one of the officers present.

The officer obeyed, putting on a pair of gloves before picking up the blouse and putting it in a clear plastic bag.

"Now," Detective Shorts directed his attention at the groundskeeper, "you said that you wanted to press charges for trespassing."

"No," replied the groundskeeper as he watched officers pull the clothes out of the garbage can and put them in evidence bags.

"Excuse me?" Detective Shorts stared at the man.

"Let them go," said the groundskeeper. "Just don't come back here."

Detective Shorts looked at Jackie, Tiny, and me, saying, "You're all free to go."

Though puzzled by the groundskeeper's sudden change of heart, I took the momentary win and followed Jackie and Tiny back to the car. It didn't make sense. He was eager to have us arrested, but seeing those clothes scared him. His whole demeanor had changed.

"I wonder why he changed his mind," Jackie whispered to me.

"I wonder why there was blood on those clothes," I whispered back.

We piled into the car and headed home, making sure that we went in the opposite direction of the parked police cars, since none of us wanted to run into Detective Shorts again. As the dark road curved in front of us, all I could think about was that garbage can, and how, without Bentley, no one would have ever known what was hidden inside of it.

Chapter 7

Loud snores woke me up. Grunting, I rolled over, still in my clothes from last night, having been too tired to bother getting undressed, and raised my head, ready to scold whomever was snoring so loud, until I realized that the horrendous sounds came from me. My tongue stuck to the top of my dry mouth and my throat screamed at me for allowing it to become so dry. I rolled out of bed and stood up, while my tangled mess of hair draped in front of my face as though it was some sort of stringy veil. I must have been quite a sight as I moseyed to the bathroom. After washing my hands, I splashed water on my face to try and wake myself up. I can't do these late nights anymore, but that never stops me from staying up.

Having finished in the bathroom, I wandered out

into the kitchen, noticing that Jackie hadn't gotten up yet. She must be more exhausted than me. I went to the coffee maker and poured a cup of freshly brewed coffee, pausing when I realized that I had never set it up last night to brew a pot when the programmable timer went off. Maybe Jackie had set it up. I didn't remember. When we got home last night, Tiny said good-bye and left. The last thing I remember was dragging my butt to bed after Jackie and I had talked half the night away as we tried to piece together the new pieces of the puzzle concerning Mrs. Paresgue's death. Before I could reach for the cream, the refrigerator opened up on its own and out came the carton of cream. I watched as the cream floated to the cabinet and out came a small dish that set itself on the counter as the carton tipped up, pouring its creamy contents into it. I reached for the cream, but it bounced through the air toward me before tipping itself up and depositing its contents into my steamy cup of coffee.

"Um… thanks," I said, assuming that it was Rachel who made this display.

"You're welcome," came her disembodied voice.

"Where were you last night?" I asked through a yawn as I sat down at the table.

Rachel appeared in a chair next to me. "I was going to ask you the same thing."

"I asked first."

"Nowhere special," replied Rachel, which made me wonder even more about what she had been up to last night. "Now your turn."

"We went to the old lady's house," I said.

"Find anything?"

"Not much, but there was this woman that was there, searching for something. And then there was the garbage can with bloody clothing in it."

"Really?"

"You are way too excited about this."

"Sorry," said Rachel. "So, was it the old woman's?"

"I assume so, but we got caught trespassing and the police showed up and made us leave."

Feeling hungry, I walked to the fridge and opened it, but my heart sank when I saw how bare it was.

"You need to go grocery shopping," said Rachel.

No kidding. I shut the fridge and went back to finish my coffee, making a mental note of all the things I needed to get done today. The water bill needed paying, and it was easier to just drive it down to city hall rather than hope that the post office would get it there on time, and now I needed to buy food.

I downed the last of my coffee and snatched my keys and phone and opened the door.

"Where are you going?" Rachel called, chasing after me.

"To buy some food," I said.

I stepped toward Greg's door and started to knock on it before stopping. He probably got in really late last night. He doesn't have the most ideal shift for his job and usually doesn't get off work until four in the morning. I didn't want to wake him if he's sleeping. Deciding it's best to let him rest, I hurried down to the parking area where my car was. Errands were just errands, and I could get them done faster by myself.

Rachel appeared in the car the moment I started the engine. "So, where to first?" she said.

"Paying the water bill," I replied. "Where's Bentley?"

"He has cream to finish. He doesn't like it too cold and usually waits for it to reach room temperature, but he was enjoying it when I left."

"How can—you know what, never mind."

I stopped myself from asking the obvious question: how does a ghost cat drink milk? But then I remembered the Halloween party that Rachel had followed Jackie and me to and how she somehow managed to get drunk off of champagne. Better to just let the poor cat do what he wants.

I reached city hall—it only took about 20 minutes—and parked on the side of the street, in the first available space I could find. As I tried to parallel park, the car behind me zipped past honking his horn and flipped me off. Seriously? It's not like I didn't signal my intention. People are in such a hurry these days. Rachel wasn't much help. She vanished from my car only to appear in the street and chucked a rock at the guy, startling a couple of people walking by who were probably wondering how this rock managed to just fly through the air on its own.

"That'll teach him," Rachel said with pride as I got out of the car.

"Do you think we can get my bill paid without attracting too much attention?" I asked.

"Why would you ask that?" replied Rachel. "I never attract attention. It's you we've got to worry about."

I headed for the entrance, but Rachel had beat me to it. She kept making the automatic doors open and close on their own.

"Look, Mel!" she screamed so that the entire city could hear her. "They installed new doors!"

They had, too. I studied the pristine doors and the glass that had no smudges at all on it as Rachel continued to toy with them. These were new. Couldn't have been here for more than a few days.

"Rachel!" I hissed as she continued to make the doors open and close on their own, having way too much fun.

A car with windows tinted beyond the legal limit drove past. I didn't know what made me stop to watch it go by, except that it seemed to have slowed down as it drove past. *Stop it, Mel*, I scolded myself. *You're being paranoid!* Most likely, the driver was just looking for a place to park close to where he wanted to go, like I did.

"Come on. I don't have all day," said Rachel, holding the door open.

"You only have eternity."

I hurried inside and headed for the second floor where the office for paying bills was. The glass doors heading into the office opened for me, courtesy of Rachel, as I walked toward them, and I jumped at one of the doors, trying to look like I had opened it myself when the cashier gave me an odd look.

"Hi," I said to the cashier, "I need to pay my water bill." I gave her the account number, which I kept stored on my phone.

Rachel picked up a pen and started playing with it as the cashier brought up my account, and I snatched it from her so that it didn't look like the pen was suddenly possessed. Rachel frowned at me blew and some air out of her mouth, causing lose strand of her hair to bounce up and down.

The cashier glanced up, but continued to look up my bill without a word. "Forty-six dollars and fifty-eight cents."

I reached for my card, but Rachel thrust my wallet into my hands. Smiling, and trying to act like everything was okay, I opened my wallet and almost gasped when I saw all of the cash in there.

"I told you I would pay you back," said Rachel.

I didn't even want to know where all of this cash came from. I pulled the out two 20s and a ten and hand-ed them to the cashier who gave me back my change and a receipt.

"Have a nice day," she said as I left.

I hurried out of city hall, with Rachel right behind me, skipping and whistling a jolly tune. Once I left the building, I spotted the same car with the tinted windows. I guessed he had found a place to park after all.

"Where to next?" asked Rachel as I got into my car.

"The grocery store."

"I hate grocery shopping."

"I don't have anything to eat."

We arrived at the grocery store within ten minutes, and before I had even finished parking the car, Rachel had already grabbed a cart for me and waited by the entrance. Anytime someone tried to take the cart from her—it just looked like a cart sitting there by itself because, of course, Rachel remained invisible—she jerked it back out of their hands. Some looked around to see if the cart had been rigged as some sort of practical joke only to have Rachel yell at them. They couldn't get away fast enough. While hurrying to the entrance, I watched as person after person tried to grab what they thought was a lonely cart free for the taking. This should be interesting. I reached the cart, and Rachel let me have it, much to the displeasure of a woman who had tried taking the same cart only to have Rachel tell her to find her own. I just smiled at her as I wheeled it into the store, but before I got very far, Rachel decided that she wanted to push the cart.

"Don't you think it will look a little odd?" I asked her as I tried to remain in control of the cart.

"No!" came her disembodied reply.

Someone walked past me, giving me a nasty glare.

"Rachel, this really is…" I tried to say, but Rachel cut me off.

I tried to pull the cart away from her, but Rachel refused to let go, and with one final jerk, she yanked it free of my grasp, and I went flying and crashed into the tile floor.

"Okay!" I yelled at her, though it looked like I was shouting at a cart with a mind of its own, "you win!"

I walked off, heading for the first item on my list, with the cart trailing behind me as it pushed itself, humming a gleeful tune. I must have been quite the sight being followed throughout the grocery store by a cart and wondered what the guys watching the security cameras thought. After I finished with the produce section, I headed for the baking aisle. Jackie wanted some shredded coconut for a recipe she planned on making. As I placed a package of coconut into the cart, a bag of chocolate chips fell in. Perturbed, I picked up the choco-late chips and placed them back on the shelf only to have them plop right back in. I picked them up for a second time and put them away, but something flung them right back into the cart.

"Rachel," I said in a low voice, "those are not on the list."

"Hey, every girl needs chocolate," she replied, and someone walking by with a basket looked at me before hurrying away.

"I'm trying to eat more healthy," I said.

"You have lettuce right there." The lettuce moved a bit. "So, you should reward yourself with chocolate."

Frustrated, I picked up the bag of chocolate chips, but Rachel grabbed onto it as well. Before I knew it, we both were fighting over this bag with me trying to put it away and her trying to put it in the cart. I pulled, but Rachell yanked harder and the bag ripped apart, send-ing us both flying. Well, more me than Rachel, who laughed so loud that several people approached to see what the commotion was. All they found was me laying on the floor covered in chocolate chips with a torn bag in my hands, while Rachel's hysterical laughter filled the whole area.

Someone kill me now, please.

Mortified, I got up and brushed myself off while placing the torn bag of chocolate chips in the cart and walked away, pretending to pull the cart after me while Rachel steered it. As I hurried away, I could have sworn that I heard a couple more bags of chocolate chips get thrown into the cart.

I tried to get out of the store as fast as I could, but another problem presented itself when we reached the dairy aisle. I had turned my back for five seconds and Rachel filled the cart with carton after carton of cream.

"What are you doing?" I demanded, forgetting that no one else could see Rachel.

A man glared at me as he hurried past, probably thinking that I was off my rocker, though he probably wasn't too far from the truth.

"Bentley needs cream," said Rachel with her arms folded.

"How much cream could a cat possibly need?" Not to mention the fact that he wasn't alive.

"Enough for eternity," replied Rachel.

"That was very good," said a woman who must have been watching the entire exchange between Rachel and me.

"Huh?" I asked, bewildered.

"The way you are able to throw your voice. It's amazing."

"What?" I said again, not understanding what this woman was talking about, while uncontrollable laughter seized Rachel.

"She thinks you're a ventriloquist!" Rachel blurted out.

Great. I just wanted to get a few groceries and instead, I am attracting all sorts of unwanted attention.

"Uh, no," I said to the woman and ran off, heading for the check out, just wanting to get out of here. The squeaky wheels of a cart chased after me.

"Wait up!" yelled Rachel.

I managed to get through the checkout line without too many mishaps, which is a minor miracle considering everything that had happened before. Of course, Rachel decided to unload the cart for me, which made the cashier a little nervous as items placed themselves on the conveyor belt all on their own. I just smiled. What else could I do?

"That will be," the cashier said in an anxious voice as plastic bags loaded themselves and floated into my cart, "one hundred and twenty-one dollars and eighty-nine cents."

I glanced at Rachel who continued to hum a merry tune while she packed my groceries for me, unaware, or just not caring, that no one else could see her but me.

Once I had my total, I paid the bill and got the heck out of there, with Rachel still pushing the cart full of groceries. I probably won't be able to go back into that store again.

Once we reached my car, I stopped. Parked in the next row over was the same car with the overly tinted windows. The first two times I saw it, I was willing to pass it off as coincidence, but this is the third time it has appeared where I am at.

"What is it?" asked Rachel as she loaded the groceries into the trunk of my car.

"That car," I said. "I swear it's following me."

"You're just imagining things."

"Maybe."

I helped her put the rest of the groceries away, and after we had finished, Rachel pushed the cart to the cart rack.

Relieved to be out of the store, I headed home as Rachel materialized in the passenger seat.

"So where to next?" she asked.

"Home," I said.

"Stop the car!"

Scaring the daylights out of me, I slammed on the brakes, receiving a series of angry honks from the guy behind me as he blew his horn over and over.

"What?"

"There's a bridal shop right over there."

"That's why you made me stop? You scared the…"

"You need a dress."

"I have groceries in the car."

"It's cold enough outside. They won't spoil."

"Rach—"

The guy behind me blared his horn as he flung obscenities my way.

Rachel jumped out of the car. "Hey, back off, man!"

I buried my face into the steering wheel as Rachel pounded her fists on the hood of the guy's car, screaming at him. I didn't what he thought, but I knew that all he saw was thin air as dents appeared on the hood of his car all on their own.

"Come on, let's go," Rachel said to me as she got back into the car.

I started to drive away, but Rachel was insistent that I do things her way.

"To the bridal shop," she said.

Knowing I would never get out of it, I just did as she asked and parked in front of the bridal shop.

The bell at the top of the door dinged as I opened it and walked inside of the quaint little place, with mannequins dressed in wedding gowns dispersed throughout the place. I marveled at the satin fabric and embroidered floral detail on some, while others had beading threaded throughout the entire gown. As I wandered through the store, I tripped over the train of one, almost knocking over the mannequin next to it.

"Look at all this stuff," said Rachel, still remaining invisible to the world. "You've got to be able to find something here."

I hope so. I hadn't even thought about wedding dresses yet. Greg and I were waiting until we both graduated, which might be awhile, and the thought of planning a wedding was a little overwhelming. Let's face it. I don't do well planning parties and everything that goes with it. It's more Jackie's thing.

"You need to try this on!"

Rachel popped up next to a mannequin with a mermaid style dress and sweetheart neckline, and enough beading on it to make it look as though it had stars sewn on it. Everywhere I went, the dress caught the light in such a way that it almost blinded me. Rachel must have read the look on my face.

"What?"

"Too much pizazz," I said.

"May I help you?" asked a woman dressed in a black day dress, accentuated by a red belt around her waist. Her curled hair and pearls reminded me of a character from a 90s movie, but I could not think of which one.

"Yes, um, I need a wedding dress," I said.

"When is the big day?" asked the woman.

"I don't know."

"You don't know when your wedding is?" she asked, surprised.

"We haven't set a date yet."

The woman's lips pressed into a thin line in disapproval.

Maybe all brides have been panning their wedding since they were six, and therefore never hesitated when it came to setting an official date.

"Do you have a particular style in mind?" asked the woman.

"No," I replied. I didn't wear dresses much and couldn't tell you most of the styles there were. Again, that was more Jackie's thing, and I kind of thought she would be helping me pick a dress, but I hadn't counted on Rachel's spontaneity.

Undeterred in helping a potential client, the woman walked me over to the changing rooms and grabbed me a robe to wear. "Though small, we have many styles to cater to our brides' differing interests," she said.

She turned to go to the shelves to find some dresses when one appeared in her hand. Confused, the woman stared at it, wondering where it had come from or if she had actually grabbed it herself.

"Why don't you try this?" she said to me.

I went into the changing room and tried it on, with Rachel in the background laughing. What was she up to? Before the woman could help me put the dress on, Rachel appeared and fastened it for me, or tried to fasten it for me. It was so tight, that I thought my ribs would break from her efforts to button all of the buttons.

"Suck it in!" Rachel said to me, garnering a confused and frightened look from the woman.

Great. Rachel was still invisible.

"I can't," I said, trying to keep my voice low, but let's face it: it looked like I was talking to myself.

"Would you like a different dress?" asked the woman, unsure of what to make of this scene where an invisible force pushed me around in an effort to get me into a dress three sizes too small.

"Maybe you should lay off the cookies," Rachel said when the woman left.

"You're the one that kept putting chocolate in the cart," I retorted.

Rachel bunched her eyebrows together. "Fine, the size might be a little small—"

"I can't breathe."

"—but it totally brings out your eyes! You have to go look in a mirror."

Rachel shoved me out of the dressing room, with me tripping over my own feet, and almost toppling over, and to an area with three full length mirrors that allowed me to see all the angles of the dress. Giddy with excitement, she twirled me around to get a good look at me, while my stomach turned as I became a little dizzy.

"You look so gorgeous!" Rachel said.

I said nothing. My dumbfounded face wrinkled in dislike and confusion, as I tried to regain my balance after being spun around for over a minute.

"What?" asked Rachel.

"I don't like it," I said.

It wasn't a bad dress, but the bodice had so much beading on it that it made it difficult to move, not to mention the ballgown like skirt, with more beading sewn into it, that kept tripping me. It was heavy and not me.

"It's too fancy," I said. "I prefer something simpler and not so heavy."

"I like beading," said Rachel.

"But you're not wearing the dress."

Rachel's face saddened, and I regretted my words the moment I said them.

"Rachel, I didn't mean…"

She disappeared, leaving me alone in front of three mirrors in something that squeezed my lungs into mush.

"There you are," said the woman, and I had forgotten all about her.

"Do you not like the dress?" she asked, reading my face.

"No," I replied, "it's a little too fancy."

"Let's get you back into the dressing room. I have three other picks for you that are more slimming and with less beading."

The woman steered me back into the dressing room, acting as though Rachel's attempt to get me into a dress had never happened.

The first dress I rejected right away. It was pretty, but too plain and looked more like a nightgown than a wedding dress. The second one was better: mermaid style, and relied on lace to dress it up instead of beading, but the skirt was so tight I could not move my legs, which made me feel like a literal mermaid. If they had dyed the skirt part green and the top purple, I would look like Ariel, minus the red hair.

"This is better, but I can't move," I said.

Remaining professional, the woman helped me out of the dress and into the third one. I wondered how many times she had to help brides go through dress after dress, until they found just the right one. In fact, the consultant seemed unsurprised that I had rejected three dresses so far.

I stared at myself in the mirror when I put the third

dress on. The A-line silhouette looked spectacular on me, giving it that classic flare with a skirt that flowed and allowed movement, and I liked the off-the-shoulder sleeves. The beading along the scooped-neck neckline was beautiful, but the bodice had silver embroidery forming a braided weave that gave it that exquisite look without weighing it down or making it difficult to breathe. This dress was a top contender.

"You like this one," said the woman, in a tone that conveyed she knew this would be a good pick.

"Yes," I said, still amazed that I was engaged.

"Let's take you out to the floor."

The woman led me to the same three mirrors outside the dressing room so that I could get a good look at myself. I twirled a little, taking in the entirety of the dress. Everything about it was perfect, except for the gigantic bow in the back. Remove that, and I would be content.

"Okay, so I am starting to see what you mean by this dress being heavy," said Rachel as she walked into the room wearing the same dress she had me try on earlier. The only problem was, it looked as though the dress walked on its own as she moved around in it, swishing the skirt from side to side. "Who knew that so much detail could weigh it down?"

Rachel stopped when she realized the awkward silence surrounding us, and I pointed at the woman whose face had gone ashen as her mouth quivered in an effort to keep a scream in. Before either of us could do or say anything, a bloodcurdling scream echoed around us as the woman jumped back into a couple of mannequins, knocking them down as she tangled herself up in the gowns they wore. Still screaming, she jumped up and ran off, but a veil had gotten tangled around her left ankle and she dragged it behind her with each step she took.

Knowing that we needed to leave, I hurried to the changing room and put my own clothes back on, throwing the dress on a chair as I left. As I ran out of the shop, I heard the woman on the phone, demanding that the police show up and protect her from evil spirits.

"Come on, Rachel!" I yelled as I rushed out the door, while Rachel busied herself with looking at some jewelry, while she waited for me to change.

Once outside, I took a deep sigh of relief, and headed for the car, knowing that I will never be allowed to enter that bridal shop ever again.

"It's probably for the best," said Rachel. "Her stuff was overpriced anyway."

I just shook my head. "Did you have to try on the dress?" I asked.

"No," replied Rachel, "but I wasn't going to let you have all the fun."

I stopped in the middle of the sidewalk, about half-way to my car.

"What?" said Rachel, annoyed.

For the fourth time today, I saw the same car with the tinted windows, parked so that the driver could get a clear view of me. Twice at city hall, the grocery store, and now here? This is no coincidence. I ran for the car.

"Hey!" I screamed as I rushed for the vehicle. "Why are you following me?"

The driver put the car in reverse and pulled out of its parking space, before coming to a screeching halt and taking off down the street, squealing its tires as it went.

"Hey!" I yelled again, but it was no use. Whomever that was, he was determined to remain anonymous. But who was following me and why?

"What's wrong?" asked Rachel, catching up with me.

"That car is following me," I said, pointing at where the car had been. "And..."

"Talking to yourself now?"

I recognized that voice, and I wished she would just go away and leave me alone.

"Jillian," I spat. "What are doing here?"

"Just happened to be in the neighborhood," she replied in an innocent tone.

"That's been happening a lot," I said.

"Coincidence."

"Some people call that stalking."

"You might want to be careful about chasing after cars and screaming at thin air while in public. Some people might think you have lost your senses."

"Seriously, lady," said Rachel, "do you ever give up?"

Jillian's face changed from smug to bewildered. At first, I thought that she had finally heard Rachel, but then I realized that she actually saw Rachel. Rachel noticed it too.

"She can see me?" said Rachel in a giddy tone. "She can see me! Well, it's about time. What do I have to do to get your attention? Moving furniture, stacking dishes on the counter, writing on your mirror—all of that went over your head!"

"Rachel…" I said out the side of my mouth as we began to attract a crowd.

She realized it as well, and closed the distance between her and Jillian before, saying, "Leave my friend alone."

We both hurried for my car, leaving Jillian alone on the sidewalk to ponder what had just happened. I was just glad to see that smug look of hers wiped off her face.

"You've been writing on her mirror?" I asked Rachel.

"I get bored sometimes," Rachel replied.

I laughed, imagining Jillian's reaction to having her stuff moved around or finding writing on her bathroom mirror.

"I should go help that poor woman clean up her store," Rachel said as I got into the car.

"I don't think that's a good—"

Rachel disappeared.

"—idea."

Well, Rachel was Rachel and would do what she wanted. Clean.

Mrs. Paresgue had a very clean home. The only way it could be that clean was if she had someone come and do it for her. Considering her age and physical limitations, I doubt that she cleaned it herself. But how would I… A name was mentioned between the woman and groundskeeper when Jackie, Tiny, and I broke into the house and eavesdropped on their conversation. What was that name again?

Maria!

But Maria who?

I needed Jack's help, but he wasn't too willing to help these days and had been ignoring Greg's calls as well. But I knew who could convince him to help me.

I dialed Tiny's number, and he picked up within seconds. "Hey, Mel, I was just thinking about you."

"Can you meet me at Jack's in about an hour?" I asked.

"What for?"

"I need him to give me some information."

"Done."

I hung up and started my car, knowing just what sort of reception I would get at Jack's, but first, I needed to get these groceries home.

Chapter  8

I arrived at Jack's apartment within the hour, having stopped by my own place to put the groceries away and explain to Jackie what I was up to, while asking her to let Greg know if he asks. She just waved me away, telling me to have fun, while playing with Bentley, though it just looked like some unseen force batted at the string she held. Got to love Jackie. She doesn't even worry about the occasional ghost showing up. As I reached for the door to the hallway that led to Jack's apartment door, I paused, took a deep breath, and tried to think of what I would say to convince him to help me.

Tiny waited for me on the other side. "So, what's the plan"

There wasn't one. I had no idea what I was going to say to Jack. All I knew was what was said about the maid while I was at Mrs. Paresgue's place led me to believe that she was my next best clue.

I knocked on the door.

No. answer.

I knocked again.

Still no answer.

"Maybe he isn't home," suggested Tiny.

"His car is parked outside," I replied.

I heard movement inside.

"Jack, I know you are in there!" I yelled through the door.

"Can't you people leave me alone," he said.

"Please open the door," I replied.

Growing tired of the exchange between Jack and me, Tiny pulled out a small pouch with some tools in it and picked the lock. He had the door open in seconds and waved me through.

I stepped inside and almost ran out the moment I saw the state of his apartment. Jack was never much of a housekeeper, but this would make the rodents want to leave. Empty, disposable drink containers littered the floor, mixed in among ketchup stained wrappers, empty bags of chips, cookie containers, and half-melted ice cream. Jack laid on the couch coated in empty Chinese boxes with a pizza box on top as a finishing touch.

"What the…" I began, not believing what I saw.

"Go away!" yelled Jack. "I'll throw you out!" He stopped the moment he noticed Tiny standing in the room with his arms crossed.

"Jack, what is going on?" I asked.

"She dumped me!" wailed Jack.

"Who?" I had no idea that Jack was even dating some-one. He never told Greg and me much, but I should think he would tell us if he was in a relationship with someone.

"This girl I met on the internet," said Jack.

"Were you two dating long?" I asked.

"Two weeks."

Tiny snorted, but held it in when I glared at him before wandering into the kitchen.

"That's... um... not..." I said.

"I just wanted to meet in person," continued Jack. "We connected so well. I thought we had something go-ing. But she left me for someone else!"

"And when did she dump you?" I asked.

"This morning!" Jack held the pizza box up to his face to dry his tears.

"Dude, you got like a science experiment, or some-thing, in your fridge," said Tiny.

The entire apartment was a science experiment.

"Jack, I really need you to focus," I said.

"You just want me to look stuff up for you," accused Jack, though he wasn't far from the truth.

"Okay, yes, that is why I am here, but this poor old woman died and she was all alone. She had no family, except a cat, and it's looking like it wasn't an accident. Don't you want to help learn what really happened so she can rest in peace?"

"No one cares if I rest in peace!" continued Jack in self-pity.

"Jack, did you ever meet her in person?" I asked.

"No," he replied.

"Then you weren't really in a relationship. A woman who doesn't want to meet you in person is not worth it, and drowning your sorrows in food is not healthy."

"But she seemed so perfect."

"Which is why it is better that you found out now that she wasn't."

"Look, man," said Tiny, interrupting us, "this woman did you a favor. This place is a dump. She would have left you anyway after seeing all this."

"You just don't understand," said Jack, rolling over on the couch.

"Okay then." Tiny walked over to the computer in the room and dropped the mouse on the floor.

"What are you doing?" demanded Jack.

"If you're done living, you don't need this," said Tiny.

"Tiny, I don't…" I began.

Tiny lifted his hand, silencing me. I didn't know what he was up to, but he seemed to have had Jack figured out.

"So, I guess I will just take this and throw it away." Tiny lifted up the all-in-one computer, but before he managed to take one step, Jack had jumped off the couch, screaming at him to stop.

"All right! I'll help you," said Jack. "I don't want some old lady to have died alone with no one caring about what happened."

Tiny put the computer back down and picked up the mouse, handing it to Jack.

"What am I looking for?" asked Jack.

"Mrs. Paresgue had a maid, and I believe that she might know something," I said.

"Wait," said Jack. "Is she that woman that died in the car accident?"

"Yeah, except it was no accident," I said.

"There were clothes covered in blood in the trash can at her house," replied Tiny.

That was all the convincing Jack needed. He pulled up screen after screen, typing so fast that I could not keep up. "She had two nieces," said Jack.

"Really?" I asked. "The paper never said anything about them."

"Maybe they weren't close," said Tiny. "Besides, you know how journalists don't always fully research stuff. They're so desperate to be the first to publish a story. It will probably get added in her obituary."

This is true. The only publication I read about her death was no more than a paragraph.

"Her nieces live in town," said Jack. "But as for…"—he continued scrolling through window after window—"Here we go! She had a maid working for her who came every day to clean and cook her meals. The woman's name is Maria Sanchez. She immigrated to the United States and obtained her citizenship five years ago. Moved here about two years ago. Lives alone, and doesn't live that far away."

I looked at the address on the screen and wrote it down.

"You want to explain this to me?" said Tiny, holding up a trash can.

"It's a garbage can," said Jack.

"It's clean," Tiny said.

I took a closer look, and remarked at how pristine it

looked. In fact, it seemed to be the only clean thing in this entire apartment.

"There is crap all over this place," said Tiny. "The rug seems to have permanent relish stains on it, and the only clean thing in here is the garbage can? You got problems."

Tiny placed the brand-new looking trash can on the desk next to Jack.

I started to leave, but stopped. "You know, Jack, if you ever need anything, you can just call Greg and me."

"I know," murmured Jack. "Go solve your mystery."

I hurried out into the hallway, glad to be out of the chaotic mess inside.

"So, where to next?" asked Tiny as he followed after me.

"Maybe I should go alone," I said. "I don't want to scare her, and besides, I don't think he should be left alone." I glanced at Jack who slumped over his desk crying.

"Fine," Tiny relented. "I'll babysit him for now, but I'm not cleaning this up."

"Thank you," I said and rushed outside to my car, hoping that the maid could tell me why Mrs. Paresgue was driving on a terrible night when she couldn't physically drive anyway.

Chapter 9

I steered my car through the winding neighborhood road, hoping that I hadn't taken a wrong turn, while glancing at the paper I had written the maid's address on, reminding myself what her house number was. It had to be here somewhere. I made another turn. I spotted a woman getting a package out of her mailbox, which had the very street number I searched for. I pulled up on the curb and stopped the car, trying not to startle the woman.

"Maria Sanchez?" I asked, trying to not sound like I was some sort of creep or about to do something to her.

It didn't work. I didn't know her and she didn't know me. Besides, we all get cautious when some stranger walks up to us and seems to know our name. Maria took two steps back, giving me a wary look, so I maintained my distance, trying to reassure here that I was not here for some sort of nefarious purpose.

"May I help you?" she asked.

I opened my mouth and shut it. I had no idea what to say! I was so busy trying to find her address, that I didn't bother thinking about what I would say. I didn't know her, and I didn't know Mrs. Paresgue. I guessed I could just try the truth, despite how crazy it sounded.

"I know you don't know me," I said, maintaining my distance so as not to scare her, "but I am trying to find out what happened to the lady you worked for: Mrs. Paresgue."

"She died in a car accident," said Maria, walking away, probably thinking that I was some sort of reporter, or blogger, looking for a story, no matter how pathetic it was.

"But she didn't drive much anymore because of health concerns."

Maria walked away.

I chased after her, desperate to get answers to my questions.

"You worked for her for the last two years," I said. "You knew she couldn't drive anymore, yet she was out in the early hours of the morning, on a road she had never been on before, in the rain. Why?"

"Contrary to what you all believe," said Maria, "I didn't know everything about her or what she did."

"But you have your suspicions," I said.

I saw it in her face when I mentioned the lonely road and the rain. The woman didn't fully believe that her employer being out there like that was an accident.

"I just want to know what happened," I said.

"Why do you care?" Maria rounded on me, waving the package in her hands, giving me a glimpse of the handwriting on the address label. It looked familiar. I know I had seen that handwriting before, but I couldn't place it.

Maria's frustrated sigh, jerked me out of my efforts to remember something. I thought about what I would tell her, what I could tell her, and decided on the truth, despite how crazy it sounded.

"Her cat came to my apartment the other day and won't leave me alone. It seems he believes that the accident isn't as it seems, and I can tell that you believe the same."

Maria gave me a doubtful look before hurrying to her front door and opening it. "Leave me alone," she said as she slammed the door shut.

Well, that went about as well as could be expected. I don't know what I thought would happen. I'd slam the door in my face too if I was her. But the handwriting on that package—I knew I had seen it before.

I went back to my car and started the engine, wondering what to do next. I glanced at the clock. Oh, darn it! I missed my class. I got so caught up in learning more about Mrs. Paresgue, that I forgot about my afternoon class. Too late to do anything about it now.

Since I did not have to work today, and there was no point in trying to get to the last few minutes of my class, I went home, though I stopped by a fast food place first. I walked down the hallway to my apartment, balancing two bags full of sandwiches and fries and a tray full of drinks. I stopped at Greg's door and knocked. There was no way I was going to be able to unlock it with my arms full, and he should have been up by now. He opened right away.

"Hey," I said, giving him a kiss. "Can you take one of these? I brought you some lunch."

He took the bags from me as I stepped inside and closed the door.

"Did you sleep well?" I asked.

"All right."

"I can go if you are still tired," I said.

"Don't worry about," replied Greg. "I'm more hungry than tired right now. What did you get?"

"Just some beef sandwiches and some fries."

He grabbed a sandwich and started eating it, while I grabbed a plate and put my food on it, trying to be a bit more civilized.

"I think we should take Jack out or something. He seems to be having a hard time," I said.

"What makes you say that?"

How could I put this? Greg didn't know anything about the maid or the fact that I had gone over to talk with her. "I saw him this morning, and he was all out of sorts. It seems that he was seeing someone and she broke up with him."

Greg burst out laughing.

I glared at him. "It's not funny. Jack seems really upset."

"Mel, I'm sorry," said Greg. "When you know him as long as I have, you'll know that he is always seeing some girl and she always breaks up with him. Was it over the internet?"

"Yes."

"There you go. Jack is always chatting with people online at these online dating sites. They go out for a few weeks, but they never meet in person. He always falls head over heels for them, but it always ends the same, with the girl dumping him. I don't know why he does that instead of trying to meet people in person. He'll be depressed for a few days and then move on as though nothing has happened."

"You're a little blasé about this," I said.

"I'm sorry. This happened when we were in high school as well. Jack would fall madly in love with some girl, and she would dump him, and he would spend the next several days wallowing in self-pity."

I put my hands on my hips.

"If it will make you feel any better," said Greg, "I will check on him tomorrow."

I handed Greg some fries. "I need to use your computer."

"What's wrong with your laptop?"

"It's in my room, in my apartment."

"You know where it is," said Greg, shoving a bunch of fries into his mouth.

"Thanks," I said, giving him a kiss.

I scooted a chair up to his computer and turned it on. My class had an online forum that students could access to find out what assignments were due and what they might have missed if they missed a class. Since I missed my class, I needed to know if I missed anything important. I logged into the forum and scrolled through the various posts, but didn't find much of anything important. Just as I was about to close the page, something jumped onto the keyboard, punching a bunch of keys, before skittering away.

A meow told me who it was. I turned toward Bentley, and watched him as he washed his face, pretending to be all innocent. I moved the cursor to the close the page, but before I could, Bentley jumped on my hand, forcing me to click something else, and a new page to pop up. He walked in front of the screen, stopping when he had passed, but his tail still rested on the monitor and seemed to be tapping the screen.

I moved Bentley's tail and read the top of the page.

Bingo Tonight at the Civic Center. Bring a friend.

"Is this important, or something?" I asked Bentley.

In response to my question, Bentley rubbed against my chin before moving to the hand I had on the mouse and nudging it, until the cursor moved to a picture of an elderly woman. I looked closer at the image. It was Mrs. Paresgue. Did she run bingo night at the civic center?

"Do you want me to go there?" I asked the cat.

Bentley purred and rubbed his chin on mine.

I took it as a yes.

"Hun," I asked, turning off the computer, "do you feel up to going to bingo?"

"Bingo?" Greg gave me an odd look. "Isn't that something old people go to?"

"It doesn't have to be."

Okay, he wasn't buying my sudden interest in Bingo.

"This wouldn't have anything to do with the old lady that died in some mysterious car accident, would it?"

He knew me too well.

"Possibly," I said.

"Can I finish my sandwich first?" asked Greg.

"Yeah. It's not until this evening anyway, which gives you enough time for a shower."

"Fine, but only if we go out for ice cream afterward."

"We'll have to get some for Bentley."

"Bentley?"

That's right. I haven't had a chance to talk to Greg ever since Bentley showed up at my door. "Did I tell you about the ghost cat that showed up at my door yesterday?"

"And the cat is…"

"Mrs. Paresgue's cat."

"I hope he likes vanilla."

Greg finished the last bite of his sandwich and headed for the bathroom, while I cleaned up the dishes and trash from our meal, wondering why Bentley wanted me to go to bingo night. I hoped it was worth it. The cat just stared at me with that look that said I should just do his bidding, trust him, and be glad that he chose to deign me with his presence.

"I hope you know what you're doing," I told him.

He just meowed and rolled onto his back, begging me to pet him.

"You know," I said, rubbing his belly, "I never really liked Bingo."

Chapter 10

Greg and I walked through the doors into the civic center and followed the signs for bingo night. Idle chatter reached my ears as we wandered into the room with tables set up in rows while a giant ball filled with cubes with numbers on them stood in the front of the room. I had no idea where to sit as I glanced around at a bunch of retirees and some middle-aged people gossiping about this or that. Greg and I must have been the youngest people there.

"There's a spot," said Greg.

I followed hem toward the seats he had pointed out, but stopped when I noticed Bentley jump on another table and walk across some lady's card, shifting it a bit. She stared at it for a moment, wondering why it had moved on its own, before rearranging it the way she had it.

"Over there," I said, pointing at Bentley, even though Greg could not see the cat.

He didn't question me, but allowed me to lead him to the two seats that Bentley stood on, with his front paws on one and his back paws on the other. Before we had reached our chairs, an elderly gentleman tried sit in one of them, but stopped the moment a shrill screech echoed around him. As he looked around, confused, I took the chair.

"Maybe I should sit here," I said, sitting down, receiving an approving look from Bentley.

The man relented and went somewhere else.

"Do you feel as underage here as I do?" asked Greg.

I nodded.

I'll say I felt out of place. I hoped Bentley knew what he was doing. Heck, I just hoped that I understood him correctly.

"If everyone can take their seats," said the announcer, "let's get started."

I grabbed the card that was in front of me. Now what? What did Bentley want me to do?

"B-twenty-nine," called the announcer.

Nope. No B29 on my card.

"Meow."

I looked at Bentley as he meowed at me and walked across the same lady's card, scattering her chips everywhere. Taking a chance that she was the one the cat wanted me to talk to, I started a conversation.

"Um, excuse me," I said to her, "how do you play this game?"

Okay, I looked like an idiot, and the lady's odd glance told me that I looked like an idiot, but I needed to start a conversation somehow.

"Oh, it's not difficult dear," said the woman, treating me like a child. "You just place a chip on the number the announcer calls, if it's on your card, and when you get an entire row done, you call out 'bingo'."

"Thanks," I said.

"I-sixty-six," said the announcer.

I found the number on my card and placed a chip on it.

"See, you're getting it," said the woman.

Greg smirked.

My mind argued with itself over how to steer the conversation over to Mrs. Paresgue. After deliberating, and turning down one idea after another, I decided to just take the plunge and dive right in, hoping that my gamble would pay off.

"Um…" I began, "I don't see Mrs. Paresgue here."

"Did you know her?" asked the woman.

"No," I replied, "but I saw her name and picture on the sign out front and I just thought…"

My voice trailed off. I don't know what I thought, or where I was going with this. I probably just sounded like a nosy idiot who just wanted to poke their nose into other people's business. My mind raced, trying to think of something to say, of some way to finish my statement. Lucky for me, I didn't have to because the woman finished for me.

"Didn't you hear?" she asked.

"Hear what?" said Greg, trying to help me out.

"She died in a gruesome car accident," said the lady.

"What?" I said, trying to pretend to be shocked. I don't know if my reaction came across as genuine or not, but if it didn't, the woman never said anything.

"It was terrible," continued the woman. "Don't know why she was out on such a terrible night."

Bentley moved over to Greg and pushed against his hand. Unsure of what to do, he moved his fingers to scratch the cat's ears, though it looked like he was petting thin air, but no one seemed to be paying any attention to him.

"Was she not supposed to be driving," I asked, trying to keep the woman talking.

"Oh, no. She had a license but had some issues, making it where she needed someone else to drive her around, not that she ever needed to go anywhere, but… well… let's say her health hadn't been the greatest lately. She also hated being out in the rain, so for her to be out on such a horrid night makes no sense."

"It was the ghosts that made her do it," said another woman sitting next to us.

"Ghosts?" I asked. No one had said anything about ghosts, nor was there any indication that any spirits could be involved, aside from Bentley, but I don't think he would hurt his owner.

"Stop that, Millie," snapped the woman. "Such nonsense!"

"It's not nonsense," said Millie.

I watched the two women argue back and forth, listening to anything they said, hoping it could be a clue.

"There are no such things as ghosts," said the first woman.

Greg coughed. I knew what he thought: better not let Rachel hear you say that because she just might follow you home to prove to you just how wrong you are.

"Mrs. Paresgue didn't think so," said Millie.

The other woman snorted.

Millie looked at me and continued. "She wasn't crazy or anything, and like most of us, thought the idea of ghosts was ludicrous—children's stories. However, for the last several months, Mrs. Paresgue has complained about her stuff moving around."

"Moving around?" I asked.

"Little things," said Millie. "Pens, papers, dishes, maybe a coaster—nothing significant, but enough to make one wonder if they were truly alone. There was one night she returned home to find that the clothes in her dresser had been shifted around. Not majorly. They were still in the dresser. But she was very meticulous. Always kept everything neat. One little wrinkle in her shirt and she would know that someone had moved it."

"So, someone was snooping around her house?" asked Greg, curious.

"More like something," replied Millie.

"Stop it," said the other woman, but Millie ignored her.

"Things got really bad a few weeks ago," said Millie. "Mrs. Paresgue complained that someone had gone through her desk and shifted her papers all around. She could never find any evidence of someone breaking into her home and both her maid and groundskeeper insisted that no one had. Yet, her stuff kept getting moved around."

"Almost like someone was searching for something," I muttered to Greg.

"She was taking medication," said the first woman. "Because of her ailments, she was on a lot of medication and one of the side effects is hallucinations."

"Hallucinations do not explain how stuff got moved

around," protested Millie. "Her maid, Maria, told me that she had come into work one day to find a file sitting on the desk, instead of being in the filing cabinet where it belonged."

"Could Mrs. Paresgue have put it there and forgotten to put it back?" I asked.

"Which is what I mentioned," said the first woman.

Millie shook her head. "She was very neat and always kept things in a particular spot in case she ever needed to find it."

The first woman looked at me. "Don't believe this nonsense. She was always neat and organized, but then her health started deteriorating and the doctors put her on a lot of medications. After that, was when she started acting erratic. I told her to get her medications looked at and adjusted, but she never listened. I mean, she wasn't always unpredictable. She had her good days, but some days it was like talking to a stranger."

"You can't always blame the pills," scolded Millie.

"It makes sense," said the first lady.

They started arguing, but before they got into it too much, I decided to bring up the bloodied blouse. "I read somewhere," I said, "about how the police found bloody clothes in a trash can at her house. Could someone have broken in and attacked her?"

Millie looked at me with a curious and concerned look on her face. This must have been the first time she had heard about it.

"Oh my gosh I almost forgot!" the first woman blurted out.

"Forgot what?" asked Millie.

"The other night, Mrs. Paresgue called me in a panic," said the first woman. "I didn't think much of it at first. She said that the ghost had shown itself to her and tried to attack her, but that she had stabbed it. Her words were garbled, and I blamed her medication. But I remember her calling me to say that she had gotten her ghost—I think she said ghost—and that she needed to get away from it."

"It?" I asked.

"I have no idea what she meant, but I told her that she was most likely dreaming and should go back to bed, but she was all excited. After a while, I said that she could come to my place if it would make her feel better. I never should have made the offer. I didn't think she would immediately get in her car and start…"

"Wait," I said, "is that why she…"

"I live out that way," replied the lady, unaware that I knew more about the accident than I had let on. "She must have been on her way to see me."

Well, that answered that question, but what was the figure she had seen that forced her out of her house?

"The maid and groundskeeper," I said, "could they be responsible for any of her weird behavior?"

"Not a chance," replied Millie. "Maria is a sweetheart and very loyal to Mrs. Paresgue. Her nieces wanted to put her in a home, but Maria wouldn't allow it, volunteering to take care of her."

"Did she know her well?" asked Greg.

"They got along very well," said the first woman. "Sometimes Mrs. Paresgue referred to Maria as the daughter she wished she'd had. And sometimes I think Maria looked upon her as a mother. Her family died years ago, poor thing. But she would never harm Mrs. Paresgue in any way. If there was one person Mrs. Paresgue trusted, it was Maria."

"And the groundskeeper?" I asked.

"Worked for Mrs. Paresgue for years. Harmless. He would never do anything to her. He was a friend to her brother and took the job to help her out."

"What about her nieces?" Greg asked.

Both Millie and the other woman mimicked spitting when he asked, making their disdain known.

"A couple of spoiled bitches, if you ask me," said Millie.

"I don't think I have ever heard you use that word," said the first woman.

"Well, it's true," said Millie. "Those two are some of the most selfish people I have ever known. They kept asking Mrs. Paresgue for money, but she finally cut them off when one of them got arrested for breaking into a pharmacy."

"Seriously?" said Greg.

"If you knew her, you wouldn't be surprised," Millie said. "Their father spoiled them rotten. I can't believe that they are going to inherit everything."

"Odd too," said the first woman. "Mrs. Paresgue had all of her affairs in order years ago, but now no one can find the will."

"Or the blue diamond," commented Millie.

Bentley's ears perked up at the mention of the diamond. At least, he seemed interested, until he started washing his face.

"Blue diamond?" I asked.

"A rare gem," said Millie. "I don't know where she got it from, but it's supposed to be worth millions."

"Oh, now," chided the first woman.

"Either way," continued Millie, "she said that it was worth a lot of money, but whenever someone asked her where she kept it, all she would say was that her most trusted friend kept it safe."

Most trusted friend? Who was that?

Bentley shoved his head against Greg's hand again, insisting on being the center of attention. He obliged, even if he did look a little silly petting thin air.

"Bingo!"

"Oh, darn it," said Millie. "I wasn't listening to any of the numbers that were called."

We all looked around to see who had called bingo, and I almost choked on the spit in my mouth when I saw Rachel jumping up and down waving a card in the air. The only problem was, all anyone else saw was a card flying around the room by itself.

"Bingo, bingo, bingo," sang Rachel, dancing around with enthusiasm. She spotted me. "Hey, Mel, I won!"

I hid my face in my hands.

"I think we should leave," I whispered to Greg, who agreed.

Bentley ran off as we stood up and snuck out of the room as Rachel continued to dance around, before walking up to the announcer and handing her the card.

The announcer took the card, her eyes wide in terror as her mouth twitched in an effort not to scream.

"You can keep the prize, though," said Rachel as she disappeared.

Greg and I hurried out of the civic center and into the parking lot. Neither of us wanted to be around when people started panicking about having seen a ghost, or something supernatural at any rate.

"So, someone was moving stuff around," said Greg.

"It sounds like they were searching for something," I replied, "but what?"

"Her will. Or maybe the blue diamond," said Greg.

Something shoved their way in between us, taking both mine and Greg's arms. "Oh, you two are so cute," said Rachel.

"Thanks," I said. "You know, you caused quite a scene."

"And it was so much fun!" said Rachel.

I looked around, hoping no one was around to see us, knowing that I was probably the only one who could see Rachel at the moment. Sometimes she would let others see her, and other times, she only let me see her.

"We should get some ice cream," suggested Rachel.

I gave her an odd glance. "Funny you should mention that. It's almost as though you were listening in on our conversation earlier."

"Me eavesdrop?" Rachel said in mock incredulity. "I'm surprised at you, Mel. Always thinking the worst of people."

"Because it's not like you've ever eavesdropped on us before," I said.

"I'm going to pretend you didn't say that," said Rachel. "I like strawberry swirl, and you're paying for it."

I looked at Greg, who shrugged his shoulders while holding back a laugh. Ice cream it was, then.

Chapter 11

A paw touched my cheek, patting it, insisting that I get up and do something. I rolled back over, pulling the covers tighter, not wanting to get up. The paw smacked my cheek again, followed by an insistent meow.

"It can't possibly be time to get up," I muttered, wishing whomever was trying to get me out of bed would go away. Greg and I had spent over half the night discussing what we had learned at bingo. Mrs. Paresgue thought her place was haunted and that she was being tormented by some unseen force. But what? And why? None of it made any sense, and before we could talk about it further, I realized that sunrise was only three hours away. Someday, I will learn to get to bed early and get a decent night's rest.

"Meow!" Bentley's harsh meow, and gentle smack,

made me open my eyes and lift my head up. Oh, crap! It eleven in the morning! I can't believe that I had slept so late. I jumped out of bed and smacked my head into my night stand as I did, still not fully awake.

"Ow!" I blurted out.

"You okay in there?" Jackie's voice came through the door.

"Fine," I replied. I wandered out into the hallway and found Jackie standing there with a cup of coffee, giving me a reprimanding look.

"Is something wrong?" I asked.

She motioned for me to follow her. Once we reached the living room, she pointed at Greg. I covered my mouth to keep from laughing out loud. Poor man was too tired to walk to his apartment next door, but the funniest part was the fact that he was splayed out over the couch with his shirt half-off, but all crooked and wrinkled, displaying some of his assets. I walked over to him and started to shake his shoulders to wake him, but never noticed the brown paper bag filling itself with air. Just as I touched Greg's left shoulder, the bag popped, causing me to jump, Jackie to slam into the wall, Bentley to hiss, and Greg sat up so fast that he clocked me on the chin and looked around with a wild look in his eyes as he tried to remember where he was. Hysterical laughter filled the room, and I knew who it was.

"Rachel!"

"You should have seen your faces!" she laughed.

Trying to calm my heart rate, I glared at her, not pleased about her joke, but Rachel was Rachel, and did as she pleased. "That wasn't funny," I told her.

"Not for you," she said.

Bentley flipped his tail and glowered at Rachel with a look that could freeze lava.

"OOO," said Rachel. "The cat is mad."

Bentley growled at her, a soft warning growl, telling her just how unhappy he was with her prank.

"Um... I have otherworldly things to do today," Rachel said, changing her tone. "Catch you later." She vanished. Sometimes, I could kill her, if such a thing was possible.

"What am I going to do with her?" I asked.

"Nothing," said Jackie, straightening her hair. "You haven't been able to do anything with her since she first showed up."

That was true enough.

"Are you all right?" I asked Greg.

"Yeah," he said, scratching his head, still confused as to why he was on my couch. "How late did we stay up?"

"Too late." I motioned for him to pull down his shirt.

He did, looking a little embarrassed, but Jackie just chuckled as she sipped her coffee.

"Who's hungry?" she said.

Before either of us could answer, she had already gone into the kitchen and grabbed the carton of eggs and a skillet. As the sizzle of eggs frying in a pan filled my ears, Bentley jumped across my laptop, turning it on. I reached for it, trying to keep him from messing up the project I was working on for my final, but before I could reach him, his rear paw touched the Windows® key, while another hit a different key, which somehow forced my computer to bring up my web browser. A part of me wondered if he actually did know how to use a computer. Maybe animals aren't as dumb as some people think, and Bentley seemed to be a bit calculating, just like a cat.

"I wish you wouldn't do that," I told him, as I reached for my computer, but he just looked at me with innocent eyes, making it so I couldn't stay mad at him.

Before I closed my laptop, an image caught my notice: it was a picture of Mrs. Paresgue with her cat in the obituary section.

> Mrs. Paresgue is to buried today. The service will begin at one in the afternoon at St. Agnes Memorial Funeral Home. All family and friends are invited to attend.

> Mrs. Paresgue is survived by her two nieces. She lived with her cat, Bentley, and had always been considered a bit of a rebel by her parents. She is best known for winning the pickled pigs' feet eating contest back in 1965. She has donated to notable causes and charities such as St. Jude hospital.

> Though she lived alone, her absence has been felt. Old family and friends have shared some fond memories of her. She will be missed.

Seriously, who wrote this? A first-year journalism student? Will be missed. Unlikely. I had never heard of her until her cat's ghost showed up at my door and it seemed that no one else knew her well either, or the ones who did have long since died, which is a shame. Pickled pigs' feet eating contest? That's something I would not want to be remembered for. I hoped someone writes a better obituary for me. It will probably read:

Mellow Summers has been a ghost magnet since she moved to our community. One particular ghost refused to leave her alone. Who knew that it would be the death of her?

Okay, maybe that one was a little morbid, but you get the gist.

I looked at the clock in the room. It's almost noon and the service was at one! This was why Bentley walked all over my computer. He wanted me to go to the service. Except, I had nothing to wear. Jeans and t-shirts were not appropriate attire for a funeral, and nothing I owned was black.

"Jackie," I called, "do you have a black outfit I could borrow?"

"Why?" asked Jackie.

"No reason."

She set a plate of eggs on the table. "Don't give me that no reason nonsense! You're planning something."

I showed her and Greg the obituary and the time of when the service was supposed to start.

Jackie pursed her lips and walked off into her room. I listened as she opened her closet and rummaged through it, searching for something. When she came out, she carried a black skirt and blouse and some ballet flats. "This should do," she said, handing me the clothes, before going back to her room. "I'll be ready in twenty."

"Ready?" I asked.

"I'm going with you, of course."

I didn't want her to have to give up her whole day just to help me out, but before I could protest, she had already closed the door to her room. Greg shoved the last bits of egg into his mouth before hurrying to the door. "I'll get changed."

"Huh?" I said, confused.

"You're not the only one who wants to know what happened to that old woman."

He left. I hadn't expected them to volunteer to go so readily, but should have known they would. I glanced at the plate of eggs Jackie had set aside for me. Guess I better eat them and get changed. Time was not on my side.

By the time I finished putting on some makeup, Jackie waltzed out of her room dressed in a sleek black dress with some silver embroidery along the neckline. It was casual, but could also serve as a cocktail dress if she wanted it to. I grabbed my coat, keys, and phone and headed out the door with Jackie. We hurried to the parking garage, and true to his word, Greg met us down there dressed in a suit, and looking sharp.

"Ladies," he said, opening the car doors for us.

Once we were all in the car, Greg drove us to the funeral home, after I gave him the address. There was no place to park except on the street, though there weren't that many people there. Enough cars lined the street, telling me that the service would have a decent crowd, but I wondered how many of these people personally knew Mrs. Paresgue, or were just there because she was a wealthy widow who met an untimely demise. More rain started to fall as we got out of the car.

"I wish this rain would stop," muttered Jackie.

I agreed. This freezing rain was tiresome and it seeped through your coat, soaking you, regardless of how well you dressed for the weather.

"We should get in before we get too wet," I told her.

People stood in their own separate groups, making idle chatter. Looking around, I didn't know where to go or what to do. I assumed Bentley showed me the obituary because he wanted me to come here, but why? I didn't know the woman and had no idea how I was to get anyone talking about her, much less whom I was supposed to talk to.

Greg offered to take Jackie's and my coat and hung them up on the line of hooks near the entrance.

"Now what?" he asked me when he returned.

Shrugging, I glanced around, trying to find an answer and spotted Millie and the other woman from Bingo. A waving tail caught my attention, and I turned just in time to see Bentley jump up on the open casket. He meowed at me.

"This way," I said.

I hurried over to the casket and stopped when I realized that a few people glanced my way, giving me nasty looks. This is a funeral, I reminded myself. I placed a hand over my mouth and pretended to be sniffling back tears. Jackie did the same, while Greg pretended to be comforting us.

"Meow!" said Bentley, causing a man next to the casket to

jump and take a few steps back. That cat could be insistent. I looked in the casket at the old woman lying there.
They had cleaned her up nicely.

"I'm surprised they release the body so early," I whispered.

"They did classify her death as an accident," replied Jackie.

"I'll send Jack a quick message," said Greg, pulling
out his phone.

My eyes settled on a lump of fur, and this time it wasn't
Bentley's spirit; it was his body nestled in Mrs. Paresgue's
arms and with a collar around his neck. Whomever had
prepared the old woman's body for burial must have done
the cat's as well. You'd never know that they were in a
terrible car accident. Poor thing. Why couldn't he move
on? What am I missing?

I looked at the collar again. Didn't I pick up a collar at the
scene of the accident? Where did this new one come from?

"You got that look on your face," said Jackie.

"Huh?"

"That look that says you're confused or trying to work
out a puzzle."

"Look," I said, pointing at the collar around Bentley's neck.

"And?" asked Jackie.

"I picked up his collar the day we went to check out the
accident site," I replied, "so how is he wearing one now?"

"She probably had more than one collar for him,"
said Jackie. "Most pet owners do that."

That made sense. And just like the family will grab
clothes for the deceased to be buried in, someone must
have grabbed the extra collar Mrs. Paresgue had for her
cat. But who would do that?

I spotted a familiar face that seemed upset that Jackie and I were near the body. Maria. Crap! I hoped she didn't give me away, but I needn't have worried because, at that moment, she ran out of the room, trying to hold back her tears, though with little success.

"She never went anywhere without that cat," said some guy, walking up behind Jackie and me.

I looked around for Maria again, but she was nowhere to be found.

"She must have loved it," said Jackie.

"She did," replied the man. "Said it was the only true family she had."

"What about her nieces?" I asked. "Seems a little odd that Mrs. Paresgue didn't think of them as family."

The man chuckled. "You don't know them, do you?"

He pointed out two women who looked like they wanted to be anywhere but here. I couldn't blame them for not wanting to be at a funeral, but they didn't look the least bit upset about their aunt's death. And one of them… I pointed her out to Jackie.

"Doesn't she look familiar?" I whispered to her.

Jackie's expression told me that she recognized the woman as the one who was in Mrs. Paresgue's house when we were there searching for answers into her death.

"They never liked her, and she never liked them," said the man, unaware of the private conversation between Jackie and me. "They are probably just glad that she is gone."

"That's a bit morbid," said Jackie.

"Sorry," said the man. "They just didn't get along."

"Meow." Bentley grew impatient with me taking so

long in figuring out what he wanted, and his impatience did not go unnoticed.

"I must be going crazy," said the man.

"What do you mean?" asked Jackie.

"I would have sworn that I heard her cat just now."

Bentley's tail twitched from side to side as he looked at me through slits, while he sat in the casket. What did he want me to do? Get rid of the guy?

"Did you know her well?" I asked.

"More or less," he replied. "I was her lawyer. I was with her a few days before she died to help her make changes to her will."

"What sort of changes?" I asked, letting curiosity get the better of me. "Sorry," I said when the man gave me a look, "I shouldn't have asked."

"All I can say is, her nieces weren't happy," he replied, "but then, they have never been happy."

"Meow!" Bentley's harsh meow shocked us all and we just looked at each at a loss for words.

"I think we need a moment alone," said Jackie, pretending to cry. She understood Bentley better than me at times.

The man walked away, nodding as though he understood our sudden emotional demeanor. Once he had gone, I looked at Bentley, who remained seated next to his own corpse.

"What do you want me to do?" I asked in in a low whisper, hoping to not draw unwanted attention.

He just meowed and pawed at his own body. Confused, I just stared at him, unsure of what to do. It seemed odd that he wanted me to touch his own dead body.

"Bentley, I…" I began, but he meowed again and pawed at something in particular that jingled each time he moved it.

"Mel," said Jackie, patting my arm, "the collar. I think he wants you to take the collar."

The collar? Why?

Before I had time to wonder as to why he wanted me to take his collar, a woman started walking toward us, and she did not look happy. Whatever I was going to do, I had to decide right then and there. I yanked the collar off the cat's body and shoved it in my bag just as the woman reached Jackie and me.

"I don't believe I know you two," she said in an accusatory tone.

"We don't know you either," quipped Jackie, having an immediate dislike for this woman.

I didn't like this lady either.

"So, what are you doing here?" the woman demanded.

"Maybe you answer that question yourself," snapped Jackie, folding her arms.

"This is my aunt," said the woman, "and I have a right…"

"You don't have a right to know anything," said Jackie, and I took a step back.

I hadn't seen Jackie get this way in quite a while, not that I blame her. This lady was ticking me off. You don't just go up to someone at a funeral and demand to know why they are there, even if Jackie, Greg, and I were there for reasons other than paying our respects to the dead.

"I could have you all thrown out," said the woman, clutching her arm, but she seemed to be cradling it or protecting it, like maybe it pained her.

"You're welcome to try," Jackie growled.

Way to go Jackie. She did not like being pushed around, and this woman was really getting on my nerves, but what most interested me was how she continued to hold her arm.

"Is your arm hurting you?" I asked, trying to break up the tension in the air and hoping to get a better look at what could be causing this woman pain.

The moment I drew attention to her arm, she jerked it back and toned down her tough girl attitude.

"If it's hurting you," I continued, "I know some stuff that will…"

"It's fine," said the woman in a harsh tone.

I backed off. Her long sleeve prevented me from being able to see why her arm hurt, but whatever it was, it was a new injury.

"Thanks for coming," the woman said, and hurried away, taking a couple glances back at me and Jackie before disappearing into another room."

"What was that about?" asked Jackie.

"See how she was holding her arm?" I asked.

"No."

"I think she hurt it and she didn't like it when I asked her about it."

"She did seem to want to get away real fast," said Jackie.

Greg came back, putting his phone away. "According to Jack, the immediate relatives insisted on having the body released so that they could bury it. Apparently, they didn't want a lengthy funeral and just wanted to move on."

"You sound like you don't believe the story," I said.

"Well, you said that bloody clothes were discovered at the old woman's house. Normally that would be enough to open an investigation, or warrant keeping the body a little longer for more forensic tests. However, the family is one of those influential ones and was very insistent that the body be released. Since, Mrs. Paresgue's death was originally ruled an accident, the D.A. was more than happy to let it go."

"He's not going to investigate further?" asked Jackie.

"He doesn't see the need," said Greg, "and the blood on the clothes you guys found, wasn't Mrs. Paresgue's."

Not hers? Whose was it, then?

"Are they not interested in the bloody clothing?" I asked.

"I don't know," said Greg. They don't know whose blood it is and, since it isn't Mrs. Paresgue's, the D.A. doesn't think he has a case and the police commissioner agrees. Jack said that Detective Shorts is angry. He wanted to continue looking into it, but has been told to back off."

"I wonder who insisted on having the body released and why," I said.

"That's the thing," continued Greg. "When I was talking to Jack, I overheard someone say that Mrs. Paresgue had a provision put in her will, where it would not be read, or have its instructions carried out until after her funeral.

"But they can't find the will," said Jackie.

"The new one," Greg said. But for all anyone knows, there never was a new will made."

"How much was she worth?" asked Jackie.

"A lot," replied Greg.

As Jackie and Greg talked, I spotted a white rose moving through a crowd of people, heading for the coffin. It wasn't the rose itself that caught my attention. It was the fact that it floated through the air on its own and a bunch of heads turned to watch it dance through the air that caught my attention. Rachel.

"Nine o'clock," I said.

"Actually, it's two in the afternoon," said Jackie, checking her watch.

"No, look!" I said, pointing at the rose as it continued its trek through the air.

"How is it…"

"How do you think?" I said.

"Well," said Jackie, "she always did love a good outing."

We all watched as the rose continued floating through the room, until it reached the casket. The various conversations in the room stopped to watch this single, white rose reach its destination. The rose floated past me.

"Rachel," I whispered, "what are you doing?"

"Paying my respects," she said.

"No one can see you," I replied.

She stopped. "Oops!" In front of everyone, for the entire world to see, Rachel materialized, with the rose still in her hand before placing it in the casket. Afterward, she faced the astonished faces watching her and said, "Hi, everybody!"

Just for kicks, Rachel vanished, leaving everyone in the room in stunned silence.

"We should go," I said to Jackie and Greg.

They agreed. While everyone stared at the empty space

that had been Rachel, the three of us hurried to the exit and ran outside, glad to be away from curious onlookers.

"I think that went well," said Rachel when we reached the car.

"You realize that you probably gave them all a heart attack," I said.

"A minor inconvenience," replied Rachel.

I raised an eyebrow at her.

"Hey, Mel, are you coming?" asked Jackie as she got in the car.

"I jumped into the back seat, wondering where Bentley had gone. Like a cat, and just like Rachel, he seemed to come and go as he pleased.

Rachel appeared in the seat next to me, causing Jackie and Greg to both jump a little. Though used to her comings and goings, she still managed to surprise us all.

"So, what are we going to do next?" asked Rachel with excitement.

I pulled the cat collar out of my purse and examined it. "I don't know."

Chapter 12

We reached our apartment complex within 30 minutes of leaving the funeral home. It didn't quite go the way I thought it would, though I didn't know what to expect. I fiddled with the cat collar, wondering why Bentley wanted me to take it. It made no sense, but the cat had been insistent. The collar itself seemed to be plain and simple. Definitely not the sort of elaborate item one would expect a woman of her stature and wealth to have. I used to read magazines about famous celebrities and the outrageous outfits they made their pets wear. This looked like a department store special. Even the little jewel on the collar resembled costume jewelry more than anything else.

We pulled into the parking area and Greg parked the

car in his usual spot. He opened the door for both me and Jackie. She winked at me when she got out, telling me that she approved.

"So, what's with the collar," asked Jackie as we all walked up a flight of stairs to the second floor.

"I'm not sure," I said, still fiddling with the collar.

"Well," said Greg, "I hope it was worth it, because I don't think we will be allowed to go back to that funeral home."

I hoped so too.

We walked through the door leading from the stairwell to our hallway and stopped. Sitting in front of my apartment door was Maria, Mrs. Paresgue's maid. She stood up the moment we entered, clutching her bag, and her swollen eyes told me that she had been crying at some point before we arrived. She stepped back as we all approached.

Not wanting to scare her further,—her fidgety nature displayed her nervousness and uneasiness at being outnumbered by so many strangers—Greg stopped and gave me a kiss. "I need to get ready for work. See you later."

"Drive safe," I told him, and he smiled, disappearing into his own apartment.

"Can we talk?" Maria whispered.

"Yeah," I replied and unlocked the door, holding it open for her.

She didn't budge. Her eyes fell on Jackie, uncomfortable with having her here. Whatever Maria had to say, she did not want to say it in front of anyone else.

"You know what," said Jackie, reading the situation, "I have some things to do. Catch ya later." She hurried down the hall, leaving me alone with Maria.

"Won't you come in?" I asked her.

Maria glanced around, a stark contrast to her more irate tone when I had first met her, and went inside. I shut the door and offered her a seat, and she sat in the giant, comfy chair.

As I walked to the couch, I noticed movement from the giant cat tree in the living room and noticed Bentley sitting up on the topmost shelf. Instead of seeming angry or frightened, like I had seen him on previous occasions around strangers, he seemed calm and very interested in Maria.

"What can I do for you?" I asked Maria, wondering why she was here, and how she found my address.

"I'm sorry if I was so rude to you earlier," she replied. "Mrs. Paresgue wasn't just an employer to me, but was more like family."

"No apology is necessary."

Bentley jumped off the cat tree and hopped into Maria's lap. She jumped a little, unsure of what was going on, but his purring seemed to set her at ease.

"I don't want to rush you," I said, trying to be delicate, "but you made it clear yesterday that you wanted nothing to do with me. What changed your mind?"

I heard ceramic cups clinking in the kitchen, not the loud kind of noise you would hear on most occasions, but a silent kind of clinking, as though the person getting the cups down was trying very hard to not make any noise. Ignoring the sounds, I smiled at Maria as she pulled a package out of her bag.

"I received this yesterday," she said.

I took the package, recognizing it as the one she had gotten out of her mailbox when I had first gone to speak with her. I opened it and pulled out an official looking paper with a note stuck to it. It read:

Maria,

You are more like family to me than anyone else and the only one I trust. Keep this safe.

Patricia

I looked at the document the note was attached to. Though not familiar with a lot of legal documents, this one looked to be a last will and testament.

"Do you know what this is?" I asked.

Maria shook her head.

I thought for a moment, trying to figure out what Mrs. Paresgue was thinking when she sent this package. I remembered the story of the diamond. "Do you know anything about a blue diamond?"

"Supposedly, she had some rare blue diamond that was given to her by her late husband. I never saw anything like it around the home and just assumed it was some story she just liked to tell to any who would listen. But this… this paints a different picture."

"Why would she send this to you?" I asked. The moment I had said it, I was afraid that Maria would think I was being rude. "I don't mean…"

"It's okay," said Maria.

Is that the coffee maker going in the kitchen? Who could be making coffee? The moment I wondered about the goings on in the kitchen, I realized that we were not alone at all, because Rachel had shown up and decided to play hostess.

"I don't know why she would send these to me, but when you came by and asked if she had been acting strange lately, I wasn't truthful when I told you no."

A tray appeared behind Maria with cups, a pot of steaming coffee, a bowl of sugar, and a small thing of cream. My eyes widened as it floated from the kitchen to the table beside Maria. She stopped talking to me and stared at the tray, confused as to how it got there.

"Coffee?" I asked, trying to sound normal.

Maria nodded.

A cup lifted itself into the air, floating to the pot of coffee, and as it did, I shook my head with such vigor that I almost made myself dizzy. When Maria looked up at me, I stopped and smiled, doing my best to act as though everything was okay.

"Help yourself," I said.

The cup landed back on the tray.

Maria picked up the cup and poured herself a cup of coffee, giving me an odd look—I had to admit; she was taking this very well—and sipped the coffee as she considered her next words.

"You had asked me if Mrs. Paresgue had been acting unusual," said Maria. "The truth is, she had been acting erratic."

"How so?" I asked.

"She seemed confused easily. Not all of the time, but

there were moments when she didn't seem to be in her right mind. I passed it off as old age catching up with her. My own mother suffered from dementia in her later years, until she died, and I was afraid the same was happening to Mrs. Paresgue."

"Was she ever diagnosed with dementia?"

"No, but her nieces passed her rantings off as the actions of a crazy old lady. But it wasn't just her actions. She seemed scared—frightened of being in her own home."

"Frightened?"

"She had confided in me once about a black shape being in her home. She said that she had seen something in black wandering around her home, going through her things. She also told me that her stuff had been moved around."

"Moved?"

"Yes, things never seemed to be where she remembered, and she wasn't the only one complaining about that. Even I noticed that some things I would put away before leaving for the night were not where I had put them the next morning."

"Could Mrs. Paresgue have moved them?"

"Unlikely. These were items that she never touched."

Mrs. Paresgue complained about seeing a black shape in her house? Could her home have been haunted? But none of that made much sense, but it would explain why she left her home in the middle of the night the day she died.

"She had also mentioned stabbing the figure," said Maria.

"What?" My head snapped up, and I focused all of my attention on her. "She stabbed someone?"

"The night she died," said Maria, "Mrs. Paresgue called

me up, saying that she had stabbed the thing in her house. Her words were so jumbled and didn't make a lot of sense. I tried to calm her down, and once she had, I told her to go to bed and that I would see her in the morning."

"You didn't seem worried about what she said?"

"No," said Maria, upset with herself, and probably berating herself for not taking Mrs. Paresgue's words mor seriously. "It wasn't the first time she had said something crazy. She was on medication that could cause hallucinations, and I had assumed that she must have had another bad dream. I should have listened!"

"You couldn't have known," I said, trying to calm her down.

Maria checked her watch. "I need to get going," she said. "I've taken too much of your time."

"It's not a problem," I said, hoping she would reconsider, but she seemed determined to leave.

Maria put her cup of coffee back on the tray and I handed her back her package. She shoved it in her bag, thanked me for my time, and hurried out the door.

I followed after her, walking her to the door and trying my best to be a good hostess. "You take care of yourself," I told her.

Maria nodded and disappeared down the hallway.

Before I went back into my apartment, I heard a door open and one of my neighbors came out with her dog, who seemed excited to be going out for a walk. I greeted her and noticed the collar her dog wore. It was similar to Bentley's, in that it had what looked like a jewel hanging from it, and piqued my curiosity.

"That's a fancy collar," I commented.

My neighbor smiled and chuckled a little. "Not really. I got it cheap from a department store, but that thing hanging there is a locket."

"A locket?"

"Yeah, kind of. Basically, I hide an extra key in there so, if I accidentally lock myself out of my apartment when taking him out, I can get back inside."

"Interesting."

"Well, anyway, I need to get him outside." My neighbor said good-bye as her dog dragged her down the hallway and to the exit, in a hurry to go outside and do his business.

I went back inside my apartment and stared at the door after closing it, wondering why Maria had run out in such a hurry. She had wanted to tell me about Mrs. Paresgue, but at the last minute, she wanted her privacy. Of course, the floating tray of coffee with all the fixings didn't help. I looked at the pot of coffee.

"Rachel," I said, "you can put the coffee away."

No response.

Did she just leave? That's Rachel for you. She pops in one minute and is gone the next.

"Rachel!"

Still no answer. If she was here, she chose to remain invisible. The coffee wasn't going to put itself away. So, I picked up the tray and carried it to the kitchen, placing the pot back in the coffee maker and the cream back in the refrigerator. Well, I tried to put the cream away, but Bentley jumped on the countertop and stared at me with wide, interested eyes, watching every move I made with the cream. Even though he could not physically drink the cream, he wanted to be acknowledged, and Mrs. Paresgue might have given him some every time he asked for it. I placed the cream in front of him, and he purred as he lapped at it.

"Enjoy, buddy," I said.

Feeling famished all the sudden, I decided to make a sandwich and reached for a knife to slice some bread. Jackie had bought some sourdough bread over the weekend, and it made excellent sandwiches, but you had to cut the bread into slices. The knife slipped. In my frantic efforts to catch it, I cut myself and seized the kitchen towel to wrap around the wound.

"Sorry, kitty," I said when Bentley ran because of my clumsiness. He poked his head out from the corner he had hidden in and went back to his cream.

As I pressed the towel on my cut, I paused for a moment and looked at the knife. Maria had mentioned that Mrs. Paresgue had told her that she had stabbed the strange figure that had been plaguing her home. What if she mistook a real person for a paranormal haunting? And if it was a real person that she had stabbed, that person would have reached for something to stop the bleeding, just like I had.

The blouse. It had blood on it, but it wasn't the old woman's blood. What if it was the burglar's blood? But what was he looking for? Someone wanted Mrs. Paresgue out of the house and was willing to make it look as though she had lost her mind to get her out. I just needed to know why.

I ditched the towel and ran to the bathroom for some

bandages. Once I had patched up my arm, I grabbed my coat, keys, phone, both cat collars and ran out the door. I started to go into Greg's apartment, but remembered that he was at work. I can't ask him to take a day off for me like this.

Jackie. Maybe she could help me. I dialed her number as I hurried down the hallway and to the stairwell. It went straight to voicemail. Where could she have gone?

I dialed Tiny. It also went straight to voicemail. Really? Why is it when you need help no one answers their phone?

I tried Jack, but wasn't surprised when he didn't answer. I hoped he wasn't trying to binge eat his way out of another depression.

I reached my car and got in while staring at the final number in my phone that I could call for help. He's going to kill me. I pressed the dial button, but it also went to voicemail.

"Uh, hey, detective, it's Mel," I said as I pulled out onto the road, "I'm about to get into some trouble, but I think I know what happened to Mrs. Paresgue. I'm heading there now."

Okay. No Rachel. No Jackie. No Greg. No Tiny. No Jack or Detective Shorts. Guess it's just me and a hunch.

A meow from the passenger seat caught my attention. Bentley sat there and stared at me with those intelligent eyes of his. Maybe I was finally starting to understand what he wanted. Time to find out if I was wrong.

Chapter 13

The sun had just set as I pulled up along the side of the fence that surrounded Mrs. Paresgue's property. I hoped the groundskeeper wasn't around. I didn't want to run into him again, considering I was about to trespass once again. I jumped out and locked my car, hoping that no passing cars would see it and think it strange that a vehicle was parked on the side of the road and call the cops. I didn't want to have to explain to Detective Shorts why I was here again, unless my suspicions were proven correct. Though, there was the slight problem of me leaving him a message before I drove here. Perhaps he wouldn't listen to it until after I finish testing a theory.

Once I reached the fence, I peeked through a small hole, looking for any sign that someone was here, but saw nothing. Maybe the groundskeeper was off tonight. I reached up and tried to jump up the fence, but fell right back down, crashing into the ground. Without Tiny's help, hopping the fence proved to be more difficult. Undeterred, I jumped at it again, but received the same result and a rear end that was more sore than the minute before.

"Meow."

I glanced to my right and saw Bentley sitting on the ground with a bemused look on his face, entertained at my feeble attempts to climb a fence.

"I don't suppose you know a way in," I said.

He purred and scampered off.

I scrambled to my feet and chased after him. He had to know something. Bentley ducked under logs and brush, and I almost lost him for a moment, before he turned up again and meowed at me, probably his way of telling me to hurry up. He paused by a small hole in the fence and waited for me to catch up. Once I did, he darted through the hole. Was he serious? I couldn't go through there. It was too small. I bent down and peeked through the opening, glaring at him as he sat on the other side waiting for me to hurry up and get over there. Sometimes, cats can be annoying.

Just then, I realized that I stood next to a rock, more like a boulder, big enough for me to climb, and tall enough for me to jump over the fence. All I needed to do was avoid the spikes. Okay, I took back the annoying part. Bentley knew what he was doing. I was just too impatient to try to interpret his actions. I scrambled on top of the rock and climbed over the fence, landing on the other side with a thump as I lost my footing and crashed onto my rump, again.

"Don't say anything," I told the cat as he watched me with that bored expression on his face, but his whiskers seemed to be turned up in a smile.

Taking another quick look around for the groundskeeper, I ran to the back door of the house where the pet door was. Bentley had beat me to it, not that he had to run to get there. He could just appear wherever he wanted to. I pulled both collars out of my pocket, wondering which one would unlock the pet door, and curious as to where Rachel had gone to. It's not like her to miss out on a chance to get into mischief. Aware of Bentley's impatient swishing of his tail, I put both collars next to the pet door, and it opened. Bentley disappeared through it and stared back at me from the other side. The problem was, I wasn't sure I would fit. Sure, the door was big enough for a medium-sized to large dog to go through, but I still wasn't sure if I would fit.

"Meow!"

Bentley's impatient meow told me to hurry up and the more time I wasted out here debating whether I would fit through a dog door, the better chance I had of being caught out here. Sucking up the inevitable, I got down on my hands and knees and crawled through the door, squeezing my shoulders through and not liking the way the edges of the door dug into them. Once they were inside, the rest was pretty easy as I wriggled my way through the pet door like a worm, except my pants got caught on something, and I would have sworn I heard a slight tear. Not much I could do about it now. Once in, I got up, catching my breath and wiping some sweat off my forehead. The one good thing about coming in through the pet door was the fact that the alarm never got triggered.

I glanced around the empty house as my imagination formed monsters out of the shadowed shapes that surrounded me. This place seemed so desolate without anyone else here, and every little noise seemed overexaggerated. I navigated my way through the dark, wondering where I was to go next.

"Meow!"

As though in answer to my unspoken question, Bentley sat halfway up the main staircase, staring at me, waiting for me to follow him. I did as the cat commanded. The only reason I was here was because of him, and he knew something I didn't. I headed for the staircase, trying not to trip over anything and wishing I had a flashlight, until I remembered that my phone had one. Sometimes I forgot that I lived in the 21st Century. I pulled out my phone and turned on the flashlight, just as Rachel popped in, scaring the tar out of me.

"Hey!"

I jumped, tripped over the leg of a chair, and fell backwards, landing on my rear for the third or fourth time tonight. It was probably going to be permanently bruised by now. "You've got to stop scaring me like that," I said.

"But it's so much fun," said Rachel.

"One of these days, you're going to give me a heart attack."

"And that's a bad thing because…"

"Really?" I gave a her a reproachful look.

"Oh, don't take everything so seriously," said Rachel. "I came here to help."

"You could help by not scaring the sh—"

"Did you hear something?" asked Rachel.

"Hear what?" Worry crept through me, as I thought about how the groundskeeper must have somehow known I was here.

"Got ya!"

I glared at her, and Bentley gave another impatient meow. "See? Even the cat is displeased."

Rachel folded her arms.

"Do you think you could keep an eye out? I don't need the cops getting called on me again."

"Fine," said Rachel.

"By the way, how did Maria know where I lived?" I asked her.

Rachel shrugged her shoulders.

"Rachel?"

"Someone might have accidentally, sort of, kind of, let it slip."

"You're giving my address out to strangers now?"

Instead of answering, Rachel disappeared, leaving me alone in the darkness with the ghost of the cat who once lived here.

Sighing, I climbed the stairs, following after Bentley as he ran up ahead of me, beating me to the top. Before I had a chance to ask him what was next, he had run down a hallway and into a room. You'd think he could have waited for me. I chased after him, trying not to make too much noise, even though I seemed to be alone in this gigantic house. The door to the room was closed. I tested the knob. It turned. It creaked as I opened it with care, not sure what I would find in there, but the room appeared to be empty, except for a cat sitting on the four-poster bed, waiting for me. The room was more of a suite than a standard bedroom with a sitting area and an attached bathroom, in addition to the main part of the room that had the bed, a dresser, and two night stands. Was this Mrs. Paresgue's room?

I opened the closet, finding the sort of fashionable wear popular among people in their 80s and 90s. Yep. This seemed to be her room, but what was I supposed to find in here? I scanned the room with my flashlight, but didn't know where I was supposed to concentrate my search, much less what I was supposed to find. Something rattled near the fireplace, and I headed for it, but just as I did, Bentley jumped in front of my feet, tripping me and causing me to fall flat on my face. My whole body ached as I lifted my head and glowered at him, but instead of being apologetic, Bentley just sat up straight, all proud of himself as he watched me.

"You know," I said to the cat, "if I end up in the hospital…"

Before I could finish my statement, Bentley purred and rubbed his face against my cheek, buttering me up.

"You have a weird way of showing affection," I told him.

I reached for my phone, which had fallen out of my hand, but as I grabbed it, it's light focused on a dark spot on the carpet. I moved the phone's flashlight beam around, searching the floor for any more of those dark spots, and found a trail leading to the center of the room. I tapped the spots with the tips of my fingers, feeling the crunching fibers of the carpet. Was this blood? It looked brownish, like dried blood does.

Bentley meowed again and brushed his tail against the poker near the fireplace. Listening to him, as this seemed to be his only way of speaking to me, I went over to the poker and picked it up, focusing the beam of the flashlight on it, looking for anything out of the ordinary. Something dried and crusted coated the very tip of it, as though someone had tried to clean the poker and missed a spot. I flicked at it with the edge of my fingernail.

"Bentley," I said to the cat, "is this what I think it is?"

He just purred in response before trotting over to a dark, rectangular shape underneath a table with a cat bed in front of it. I inspected it closer. It took me a moment to realize that it was a safe, but it was built into the wall and made to look like it was part of it, with a tiny nob that looked more like a notch than an actual turn dial. I focused my flashlight beam on it for a better look. Combination lock. I remembered what someone had told me: Mrs. Paresgue only trusted one person with her secrets, except, in this case, her most trusted confidant was her cat.

"Meow!" Bentley crawled up my leg and pulled at the coat pocket that had the collars in it.

I pulled them out of my pocket and studied them some more. They looked identical, and each had a sort of jewel on them, but the jewel felt hollow, costume almost, unless… What was it my neighbor had told me? That some owners like to put lockets on their pet's collars. What if Mrs. Paresgue had done the same?

I held one collar up to my light and noticed a small notch in it. Slipping the edge of my fingernail into it, I popped open the small locket, but there wasn't anything inside. Instead, it was just a series of numbers. I opened the other locket on the collar and found another series of numbers. If this was the combination to the safe, which ones do I use first? Underneath the numbers in one locket was the letter A, and underneath the numbers in the second one was the letter B. Could it be that simple?

In answer to my question, Bentley's paw grabbed the collar with the letter A out of my hands, pulling it to the floor. I decided to trust the cat on this one. I read the numbers and put them in the combination lock, turning it clockwise first. A click sounded as the lock popped free once I finished putting the final number in the second locket in. Heart pounding,—what was I going to find in here?—I opened the safe, revealing a small velvet wrapped shape. I picked it up and unwrapped it, gasping when my flashlight shone on the small blue diamond in my hand.

"So, you really were its guardian," I said to Bentley, who just stared at me as though it was about time I had figured out what he had been trying to tell me all along.

Before either of us could say anything else, footsteps sounded on the steps. Shoot! I never heard the door open! And where was Rachel? She was supposed to be keeping watch.

I ran out of the room, shoving the diamond into my pocket, but turned back around and rushed back into the bedroom just as whomever had entered the house reached the top of the stairs. Turning in circles, my mind raced, trying to figure out what I should do. I hurried to the window. Too high. My eyes settled on the closet, and though it was a bit cliched, my only other choices were the bathroom or under the bed. I wasn't about to dive under the bed and the closet was closer. Footsteps drew nearer and paused outside the bedroom door as I shut myself in the closet.

The door to the room opened and steady, but cautious, footsteps entered.

Huddled in the closet, I clutched my phone as I sent off a quick text to Tiny, knowing that he could get here in a hurry. I listened to the footsteps wander around the room as things got shuffled around. What was going on? What was the person searching for?

My phone binged, causing me to cringe as its singular, musical sound echoed around me, alerting the entire world to my presence. Why was it I never remembered to put my phone on silent? The door to the closet swung open, allowing the light in the room to reveal my presence.

"Get out," said a female voice as the barrel of a gun was pointed in my face.

Knowing I had little choice, I stepped out of the closet, recognizing the face in front of me as my eyes adjusted to the light. The woman from the funeral, Mrs. Paresgue's niece, stood in front of me.

"You," she spat, recognizing me as well. "What are you doing here?"

"I could ask you the same," I said, refusing to answer her question. As I looked at her, I recognized the coat she wore. She was here the night Jackie, Tiny, and I snuck into this house.

"I could shoot you for trespassing," she threatened.

"Really?" I said. I needed to buy time, to try and think of a plan. "You're sneaking in here in the middle of the night, which means you have no business being here."

"I inherited this place."

"No, you haven't. No yet. Not until the will has been read and the executer of the estate carries out its instructions. Officially, you own nothing."

The woman stared at me, sizing me up. It seemed that, for now, my gamble had paid off, but for how long? And where in the world was Rachel? The sleeve to the woman's coat slipped a bit, revealing a nasty gash on her arm. My suspicions about earlier were correct.

"That is quite the cut on your arm," I said, thinking about the bloody blouse in the garbage can and about what Millie and Maria had told me about Mrs. Paresgue and how she thought that some ghost was haunting her home. It was no ghost. It was the woman standing in front of me. "How long have you and your sister been haunting your aunt?"

"My sister?" asked the woman. "That idiot doesn't know up from down."

"So, it was just you then."

The woman remained silent, but I continued talking, trying to buy time for Tiny to get here.

"Scaring your aunt couldn't have been difficult. A big house like this—it's not that hard to hide in it, and you already knew the alarm code. Probably had a key, even if you had to steal it to get it."

Something shiny on the nightstand caught my eye and I eased my way toward it, trying to make my movements seem natural.

"Stay right there," commanded the woman.

"How long were you trying to make your aunt seem crazy? You must have been working on her for months."

"Three to be exact. It wasn't hard. She got put on some new medication." The woman laughed a bit. "It's almost as though the doctors wanted to help me make her look crazy. Psychosis and hallucinations were a side -effect. All I had to do was sneak into the house when she was asleep, which she spent most of her time doing these days, and move things around. To amp it up some, I would dress up in this black overcoat and stand in the shadows, and I let her mind do the rest."

I thought back to the blood-soaked blouse in the garbage can outside. "But then your aunt did something you didn't expect. She attacked you with that poker."

"Guess I did my job a little too well," said the woman.

"But that still doesn't explain why she was out..." I stopped myself as my mind worked through the events leading up Mrs. Paresgue driving on a terrible, rainy night when she shouldn't have been. "She recognized you that night she gave you that gash on your arm. That explains it. That was why she was out on that road that night. It wasn't a ghost she was running from, but you, her own flesh and blood. She must have run, grabbed Bentley, and left while you wrapped the closest thing you could find around your arm. But before she could reach her destination, she crashed, and the accident killed her and her cat, solving one loose end for you."

"That was convenient," said the woman. "Who is my aunt to you?"

"I know her cat." That was true enough. Bentley had sought me out, though I had a feeling that Rachel might have had a little something to do with that.

"That stupid cat," spat the woman. "She doted on that thing. Gave it everything, treated it better than her own family. Good riddance."

A growl mixed with a hiss came from a corner in the room. I couldn't see Bentley this time, but it sounded like him.

"But something doesn't add up," I said. "If you are so certain that you will inherit this place, why have you been searching through it? Unless, you were never going to inherit it, and there was something in here you wanted, like an authentication notice for a particular blue diamond."

"I don't know how you know all of this…"

"I told you, the cat told me," I said, in a bit of a sarcastic tone, as I reached behind me for the glass item on the nightstand.

The woman scoffed at my statement.

"This entire situation is hilarious, though," I said, trying to sound braver than I felt, and wishing Rachel, Tiny, or someone would show up and help me out of this mess.

"How's that?" asked the woman, allowing me to buy more time.

"Think about it. You have spent months searching for this diamond and have encountered one problem after another. It's kind of poetic."

"There's one problem I am about to remedy." The woman raised her gun, pointing it right at me.

It was now or never.

I snatched the glass object from the nightstand and threw it at the woman, while at the same instant, the groundskeeper burst into the room and hit the woman over the head with a shovel. She fell to the ground unconscious, and I kicked the weapon out of her hand.

"Thanks," I said to the groundskeeper.

"What are you doing back here?" he demanded, sounding a little grumpy, not that I blamed him. This entire situation was a bit of a fiasco.

"I was following a cat," I said.

He rolled his eyes.

"How did you know we were up here?" I asked.

"I was spreading salt on the driveway when a pebble hit me in the head. That's when I noticed a light on in this room, when the pace should have been dark. So, I came in here, thinking that some kids might have broken in, and that's when I heard her threaten you."

"So, you weren't…"

The groundskeeper pointed his shovel at the woman lying on the floor. "I hated that—"

Before he could finish, the roar of a bunch of bikes filled air as they tore up the driveway and parked in front of the entrance, disturbing every creature and neighbor along the way.

"Who are they?" demanded the groundskeeper when he looked out the window and saw Tiny with his entire gang.

"The cavalry," I said, trying to sound innocent. "Keep an eye on her."

I ran downstairs to stop them before they busted down the door, but, as it turned out, Rachel had beat me to it. She swung the front door open, though it looked like it had opened itself, saying, "Come on in, boys!"

Tiny ran inside, followed by Sombrero and the others. "Mel? I thought..."

"I was, but, everything's fine now," I said, as Rachel shut the door, laughing, causing a few of Tiny's men to take a step back, since none of them could see her. "We should probably call the police so they can sort this mess out."

Flashing lights appeared outside the windows.

"Already took care of that," said Rachel. "And, by the way, you are welcome."

I gave her a confused look.

"If it wasn't for me, that groundskeeper wouldn't have been here to save your little behind."

I continued to stare at her. She could have stayed with me instead of wandering off. But Rachel was Rachel.

"I think a thank you is in order," she said, with her arms crossed, though I was the only one who saw her. She liked making it where others only heard a disembodied voice.

"Thank you," I said.

Rachel beamed and gave me a giant bear hug. "You're so welcome!" She vanished.

Tiny and his men just watched the entire exchange in silence. He was used to the idea of Rachel,—she did force him to drink tea when he had a bad cold one year— and his men knew not to question it.

The police burst into the house, led by Detective Shorts. Now was the time to try and explain everything, and I had no idea how I was going to tell him that the ghost of a cat led me here.

Chapter 14

I woke up the next morning to a quiet, uneventful morning. At first, I thought that this was a hoax and expected Rachel to pop out of nowhere and scare me again, but nothing happened. After nothing happened, I got up and got dressed, certain that Rachel would stop by at some point, whether it was a few hours or a few months from now. Once dressed, I picked up the blue diamond I had gotten from Mrs. Paresgue's house, noticing a small envelope beneath it. I know I shouldn't have kept it, but something told me that Mrs. Paresgue wanted someone other than the police to have it. I shoved it in my pocket and opened the envelope, chuckling a little when I saw Rachel's handwriting. So, she did stop by after all.

Dear Mel,

You might want this, you little thief. See you at
Thanksgiving dinner.

Your Friendly Neighborhood Ghost,

Rachel

Behind the note was an authentication letter for the
diamond itself and a personal letter to Maria from Mrs.
Paresgue. I put it all back in the envelope. Yes, I supposed
I would need this. Before going to dinner at Tiny's,—last
night he had decided that we would all celebrate Thanksgiving there—I grabbed my keys, phone, and coat and
headed out the door.

"Mel, where are you going?" Jackie asked as I left.

"There's something I need to do," I said. "I'll meet
you all at Tiny's."

I hurried down to my car and started it up. The rain
had turned to snow. Perfect. Nothing like a sheet of ice
underneath a layer of fluffy snow to cause accidents.
Once on the road, I headed for Maria's, hoping that I
could catch her before she went to whatever Thanksgiving plans she might have had.

When I reached her home, I sat in my car for a moment, trying to find the right words to say. Let's face it:
we didn't exactly get off on the right foot, but I had a job
to do, and it was best to not drag it out. Clutching the
diamond and the two letters in my pocket, I walked up to

the front door and knocked. Maria answered right away, and had a look of suspicion and confusion on her face when she saw me.

"I'm not going to stay long," I said.

I pulled out the diamond, wrapped in its velvet cloth, and the envelope with the two letters in it, and handed them both to her.

"I think Mrs. Paresgue would have wanted you to have this."

She opened the envelope and pulled out both letters, reading the one that had been handwritten by the old woman herself. As she read it, a tear fell from her eye, telling me that I had done the right thing. Feeling uncomfortable standing here as she read a personal letter, I looked around and spotted Bentley in the distance, watching me. He swished his tail and vanished, having completed what he had set out to do, and saying goodbye in his own way. I was going to miss him.

"Thank you," Maria said to me.

"You're welcome." I didn't know what else to say. I started to leave, but stopped when I realized that no sounds of conversations or laughter came from her home. "Um, I know you don't know me very well, but my friends and I are having a little Thanksgiving gathering. You're welcome to join us, if you'd like. They're a rowdy bunch, but they are good people."

"I'd like that."

Maria put the diamond and letters inside, grabbed her coat, and followed me to my car. Inviting her over was the least I could do. She shouldn't be alone right now. I just hoped Rachel didn't try to make too much of an impression.

Chapter 15

"Meow!"

My eyes popped open as an incessant meow woke me from a deep, turkey induced slumber. Did I just hear what I thought I heard?

"Meow!"

Déjà vu struck me as I rolled out of bed in the middle of the night, knowing I would not be allowed to sleep until I investigated and saw what kept making that noise. I checked my clock. Three in the morning. Why is it when you wake up in the middle of the night, it almost always seems to be three in the morning?

"Meow!"

I dragged myself down the hallway and to the front door. This meow sounded different. It was more high-pitched and not as insistent as Bentley's was. I opened the front door and found a tiny, white kitten with a tan strip on his left cheek, complete with a ribbon tied into a bow around his neck, looking up at me with wide, hopeful eyes as he sat next to a bag of kitten food, two cat dishes, an empty litter box, and a bag of litter, all of which also had bows on them. Not believing what I saw, I just stared at it.

"Meow!" it said in its high-pitched voice and purred.

"Jackie!" I called, hoping this kitten wasn't the spirit of another cat. For all I knew, I just imagined this whole thing.

She came out of her room, rubbing sleep out of her eyes. "What?"

I pointed at the kitten. "This is real, right? There really is a kitten here?"

Her face lit up when she saw the kitten. "Ah, he's so cute!" She picked him up and cradled him as he purred so loud you could hear him across the room. "How could you leave him in the cold?"

"It's an enclosed hallway, and it's heated," I said, but Jackie ignored me as she hugged the kitten and cooed to it.

I picked up the bag of kitten food, the two cat dishes, the litter box, and the bag of litter, and closed the door, having a pretty good feeling how it all showed up at my door. Oh well. At least I wasn't imagining things or seeing another ghost right now.

"You're just so cute," Jackie said to the kitten.

"What do we name him?" I asked.

Jackie thought for a moment. "How about Stripes, because of his tan stipe on his cheek."

The kitten purred, as though to say that he liked the name.

"Stripes it is," I said. "Are you hungry Stripes?"

"Meow!"

About the Author

Janet McNulty currently lives in West Virginia where she continues to work on the Mellow Summers Series. She began the series two years ago as a fluke, but liked writing it so much, that she decided to stick with it.

Besides writing paranormal mysteries, Ms. McNulty has also accomplished success in other genres. She has a fantasy saga published under the name of Nova Rose, her *Dystopia Trilogy*, and a science fiction series known as the *Solaris Saga*. "A little something for everyone," she said when asked about it.

Currently, she is working on the second book in her new *Enchained Trilogy*, which is a new dystopian series.

Of course, writing is not the only passion in her life and every author needs some down time. When she isn't working on her books, Ms. McNulty enjoys reading and just poking around in her garden.

More by Janet McNulty

The Mellow Summers Series

Mellow Summers moves to Vermont to attend college, accompanied by her friend Jackie. They soon find themselves running into ghosts and one mystery after another.

Get the entire series:

Sugar And Spice And Not So Nice
Frogs, Snails, And A Lot Of Wails
An Apple A Day Keeps Murder Away
Three Little Ghosts
Oh Holy Ghost
Where Trouble Roams
Two Ghosts Haunt A Grove
Trick Or Treat Or Murder

Roses Are Red…He's Dead
Double, Double, Nothing But Trouble
Ring Around The Rosy Not Another Ghosty
Hickory Dickory Dock, The Ghost In The Clock
Violets Are Bue, More Trouble Brews
Hey Diddle Diddle, The Zombie In The Middle
Easy As Pie, Until Someone Dies

The Dystopia Trilogy

Dystopia (Book 1)
Tempered Steel (Book 2)
Liberty's Torch (Book 3)

**Imagine living in a world where
everything you do is controlled.**

Dana Ginary lives in a world where every aspect of her life is controlled by the Dystopian Government. Forced to work in Waste Management, her life becomes a nightmare with hunger and survival is her only constant. Before she knows it, she is caught up in a resistance movement and exiled from Dystopia, forced to find her way in the barren wastelands. While there, she must learn to live independently and discover how far she is willing to go to live and achieve freedom.

The Solaris Saga

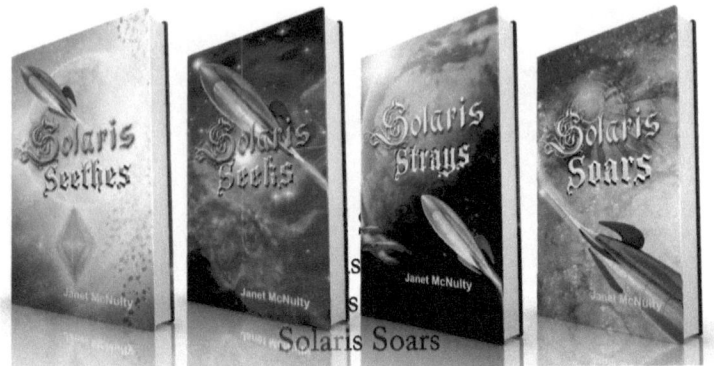

Solaris Seethes
Solaris Seeks
Solaris Strays
Solaris Soars

Every myth has a beginning

After escaping the destruction of her home planet, Lanyr, with the help of the mysterious Solaris, Rynah must put her faith in an ancient legend. Never one to believe in stories and legends, she is forced to follow the ancient tales of her people: tales that also seem to predict her current situation.

Forced to unite with four unlikely heroes from an unknown planet (the philosopher, the warrior, the lover, the inventor) in order to save the Lanyran people, Rynah and Solaris embark on an adventure that will shatter everything Rynah once believed.

The Legends Lost Series

Published under Nova Rose

Tesnayr
Amborese
Galdin

Enter the Lands of Tesnayr and join on an epic fantasy adventure that spans over 1,500 years.

Begin with Tesnayr, the first king of the five lands as he unites the against a savage foe bent on their destruction.

Next, Join Amborese as she fights reclaim the throne after her family was forced to flee from it.

Thinking peace has finally entered the land, follow Galdin as he returns to Tesnayr to find it greatly hanged. Barbarians, led by a mysterious sorcerer, burn and destroy as they go. And only Galdin can stop them if he chooses to accept his fate.

Grandpa's Stories

My grandfather grew up in Arizona during the 1920s and 1930s. One week after the attack on Pearl Harbor he joined the Navy. During the summer of 2012, my mother visited him and recorded his stories about growing up, World War II, and his time as an employee at the Pacific Bell Telephone Company. This is the history of the 20th century as he lived it. These recordings make up this book. These are his words.